THE SATYRICON
OF
PETRONIUS ARBITER

THE SATYRICON

OF

PETRONIUS ARBITER

Translation Ascribed to
OSCAR WILDE

DORSET PRESS
NEW YORK

This edition published by Dorset Press,
a division of Marboro Books Corp.

1992 Dorset Press

ISBN 0-88029-993-2

Printed and bound in the United States of America

M 9 8 7 6 5 4 3 2 1

THE SATYRICON
OF
PETRONIUS ARBITER

INTRODUCTION

TACITUS writes (Annals, XVI. chs. 17 and 18—20, A.D. 66): "Within a few days, indeed, there perished in one and the same batch, Annaeus Mela, Cerialis Anicius, Rufius Crispinus and Petronius." chs. 18—20: "With regard to Caius Petronius, his character and life merit a somewhat more particular attention. He passed his days in sleep, and nights in business, or in joy and revelry. Indolence was at once his passion and his road to fame. What others did by vigour and industry, he accomplished by his love of pleasure and luxurious ease. Unlike the men who profess to understand social enjoyment, and ruin their fortunes, he 'ed a life of expense, without profusion; an epicure, yet not a prodigal; addicted to his appetites, but with taste and judgment; a refined and elegant voluptuary. Gay and airy in his conversation, he charmed by a certain graceful negligence, the more engaging as it flowed from the natural frankness of his disposition. With all this delicacy and careless ease, he showed, when he was Governor of Bithynia, and afterwards in the year of his Consulship, that vigour of mind and softness of manners may well unite in the same person. With his love of sensuality he possessed a talent for business. From his public station he returned to his usual gratifications, fond of vice, or of pleasures that bordered upon it. His gaiety recommended him to the notice of the Prince. Being in favour at Court, and cherished as the companion of Nero in all his select parties, he was allowed to be the arbiter of taste and elegance. Without the sanction of Petronius nothing was exquisite, nothing rare or delicious.

"Hence the jealousy of Tigellinus, who dreaded a rival in the good graces of the Emperor almost his equal; in the science of luxury his superior. Tigellinus determined to work his downfall; and accordingly addressed himself to the cruelty of the Prince,—that master passion, to which all other affections and every motive were sure to give way. He charged Petronius with having lived in close intimacy with Scaevinus, the conspirator; and to give colour to that assertion, he bribed a slave to turn informer against his master. The rest of the domestics were loaded with irons. Nor was Petronius suffered to make his defence.

"Nero at that time happened to be on one of his excursions into Campania. Petronius had followed him as far as Cumae, but was not allowed to proceed further than that place. He scorned to linger in doubt and fear, and yet was not in a hurry to leave a world which he loved. He opened his veins, and closed them again, at intervals losing a small quantity of blood, then binding up the orifice as his own inclination prompted. He conversed during the whole time with his usual gaiety, never changing his habitual manner, nor talking sentences to show his contempt of death. He listened to his friends, who endeavoured to entertain him, not with grave discourses on the immortality of the soul or the moral wisdom of philosophers, but with strains of poetry and verses of a gay and natural turn. He distributed presents to some of his servants, and ordered others to be chastised. He walked out for his amusement, and even lay down to sleep. In this last scene of his life he acted with such calm tranquillity, that his death, though an act of necessity, seemed no more than the decline of nature. In his will he scorned to follow the example of others, who like himself died under the tyrant's stroke; he neither flattered the Emperor nor Tigellinus nor any of the creatures of the Court. But having written, under the fictitious names of profligate men and women, a narrative of Nero's debauchery and his new modes of vice, he had the spirit to send to the Emperor that satirical romance, sealed with his own seal,—which he took care to break, that after his death it might not be used for the destruction of any person whatever.

"Nero saw with surprise his clandestine passions and the secrets of his midnight revels laid open to the world. To whom the discovery was to be imputed still remained a doubt. Amidst his conjectures, Silia, who by her marriage with a Senator had risen into notice, occurred to his memory. This woman had often acted as procuress for the libidinous pleasures of the Prince, and lived besides in close intimacy with Petronius. Nero concluded that she had betrayed him, and for that offence ordered her into banishment, making her a sacrifice to his private resentment." (Murphy's Translation, Second edition, 1811.)

Two questions arise out of this famous passage:

1. Is Petronius (Arbiter), author of the *Satyricon*, the same person as the Caius Petronius here described, and spoken of by the Historian as "elegantiae arbiter" at the Court of Nero? 2. Is the existing *Satyricon* the "satirical romance" composed by the Emperor's victim during his dying hours and sent under seal to the tyrant?

Both points have been long and vigorously debated, but may now be taken as fairly well settled by general consent,—the answer to the first query being Yes!, to the second, No!

The Introductory Notice to Petronius, in the noble "Collection des Auteurs Latins" edited by M. Nisard, sums up the controversy thus: "Is Petronius here mentioned by Tacitus the Author of the *Satyricon*, and are we to regard this work as being the testamentary document addressed to Nero of which the Historian speaks? These two questions so long and eagerly disputed, may be looked upon as decided by this time. The Consular, the favourite of Nero, the "arbiter of taste and elegance" at the Imperial Court, is generally acknowledged to be our Petronius *Arbiter;* whose book, diversified as it is with "strains of poetry and verses of a gay and natural turn," with its tone of good company and its easy-going Epicurean morality, is so much in keeping with the cheerful, uncomplaining death of the pleasure-loving courtier who understood his master's little peculiarities, and had, like Trimalchio, adopted for his motto, "Vivamus, dum licet esse," —"Let us eat and drink, for to-morrow we die." At any rate in our own opinion, this first point is finally and definitely decided.

"Can this satire (*The Satyricon*) be the testament of irony and hate which the victim sent to his executioner? To this further question we answer No!— and our personal conviction on the point is shared by the most weighty authorities. We will limit ourselves here to one or two observations. According to Tacitus, Petronius had already caused his veins to be opened, when he started to recapitulate the series of Nero's debaucheries in this deposition. The document therefore must necessarily have been brief; whereas the work we possess, too extensive as it stands to have been composed by a dying man, was originally of much greater length, for it seems proved by the titles affixed to the Manuscripts that nearly nine-tenths of the whole is lost. Besides, Petronius had expressly limited his statement to an account of Nero's secret debaucheries, with no further disguise beyond the use of fictitious names,—'under the names of profligate men and women.' Lastly the extremely varied character of the Work is diametrically opposed to a view making it out to have been a personal libel, a piece of abuse that only stops short of giving the actual name of the individual pilloried."

What is known of Petronius himself, the man Petronius?—Granting an affirmative answer may be given to question 1, something; but even then not much.

His name was Caius Petronius; he was a Roman *Eques* or Knight, born at Massilia (Marseilles). Even these initial points are not quite firmly established;

Pliny and Plutarch speak of *Titus* Petronius, and the facts of his being an Eques and his birth at Marseilles rest on conjectural evidence. He was successively Proconsul of Bithynia, and Consul, in both which high offices he showed integrity, energy and ability.

He was in high favour at the Court of Nero, where he devoted his undoubted talents and genial wit to the amusement of the Prince, the systematic cultivation of an elegant and luxurious idleness and the elaboration of a refined profligacy. He won the title among his fellow courtiers of "arbiter elegantiae," a nickname that appears to have grown into a sort of surname, posterity knowing him universally as Petronius *Arbiter*.

Eventually he incurred the jealousy and enmity of Nero's all-powerful Minister, Tigellinus, who contrived his ruin. Informed against for conspiracy, or at any rate association with conspirators, he voluntarily opened his veins. Displaying much fortitude and a fine indifference, he died calmly and composedly, spending his last hours in merry conversation with his friends, the recitation of light-hearted verses and the composition of a candid and circumstantial account of the Emperor's debaucheries, which he sent under seal to his Master as his dying bequest.

Pliny (1) and Plutarch (2) add further touch, that previous to his death he broke to pieces a Murrhine vase of priceless value, which was amongst his possessions, to prevent its falling into the tyrant's hands.

As to his great work, the so-called *Satyricon*, its characteristics and place in Literature, we cannot do better than quote from what Prof. Ramsey says of it

in the "Dictionary of Greek and Roman Biography":
—"A very singular production, consisting of a prose
narrative interspersed with numerous pieces of poetry,
and thus resembling in form the Varronian Satire, has
come down to us in a sadly mutilated state. In the
oldest MSS. and the earliest editions it bears the title
Petronii Arbitri Saturicon, and as it now exists, is
composed of a series of fragments, the continuity of
the piece being frequently interrupted by blanks, and
the whole forming but a very small portion of the
original, which, when entire, contained at least sixteen
books, and probably many more. It is a sort of comic
romance, in which the adventures of a certain Encolpius and his companions in the south of Italy, chiefly
in Naples or its environs, are made a vehicle for exposing the false taste which prevailed upon all matters
connected with literature and the fine arts, and for
holding up to ridicule and detestation the folly, luxury
and dishonesty of all classes of the community in the
age and country in which the scene is laid. A great
variety of characters connected for the most part with
the lower ranks of life are brought upon the stage,
and support their parts with the greatest liveliness and
dramatic propriety, while every page overflows with
ironical wit and broad humour. Unfortunately the
vices of the personages introduced are depicted with
such minute fidelity that we are perpetually disgusted
by the coarseness and obscenity of the descriptions.
Indeed, if we can believe that such a book was ever
widely circulated and generally admired, that fact

alone would afford the most convincing proof of the
pollution of the epoch to which it belongs. . . .

"The longest and most important section is generally
known as the *Supper of Trimalchio*, presenting us with
a detailed and very amusing account of a fantastic
banquet, such as the most luxurious and extravagant
gourmands of the empire were wont to exhibit on their
tables. Next in interest is the well-known tale of the
Ephesian Matron, which here appears for the first time
among the popular fictions of the Western world,
although current from a very early period in the
remote regions of the East. . . . The longest of the
effusions in verse is a descriptive poem on the Civil
Wars, extending to 295 hexameter lines, affording a
good example of that declamatory tone of which the
Pharsalia is the type. We have also 65 iambic trim-
eters, depicting the capture of Troy (*Troiæ Halosis*),
and besides these several shorter morsels are interspersed replete with grace and beauty."

Teuffel in his masterly "History of Roman Literature" is brief, but to the point, in what he says of the
Satyricon:—"To Nero's time belongs also the char-
acter-novel of Petronius Arbiter, no doubt the same
Petronius whom Nero (A.D. 66) compelled to kill
himself. Originally a large work in at least 20 books,
with accounts of various adventures supposed to have
taken place during a journey, it now consists of a heap
of fragments, the most considerable of which is the
Cena Trimalchionis, being the description of a feast
given by a rich and uneducated upstart. Though
steeped in obscenity, this novel is not only highly im-

portant for the history of manners and language, especially the plebeian speech, but it is also a work of art
in its way, full of spirit, fine insight into human nature,
wit of a high order and genial humour. In its form
it is a *satira Menippea,* in which the metrical pieces
interspersed contain chiefly parodies of certain fashions
of taste."

"The narrator and hero of the romance," Nisard
writes in the Preliminary Notice to "Petronius" in the
Collection des Auteurs Latins, "is a sort of Guzman
d'Alfarache, a young profligate, over head and ears
in debt, without either fortune, or family, and reduced,
with all his brilliant qualities, to live from hand to
mouth by dint of a series of more or less hazardous
expedients. The pictures he draws with such a bold
and lifelike touch change and shift without plan or
purpose, following each other with the same abrupt
inconsequence we observe in real life; and we are
strongly tempted to conclude Petronius has largely
depicted in them the actual phases of his own, that of
a self-made adventurer, appropriating as his own with
extraordinary success the tone of persiflage and the
ironical outlook on existence of a man of high birth
and station. With equal ease he sounds the most con-
tradictory notes. Verse and prose, precepts of rhetoric
and of ethics, scenes of profligate indulgence, comic
descriptions of a feast where luxury is carried to
ludicrous extremes, anecdotes told in the happiest
manner, notably the world-famous tale of the Ephesian
Matron, epic poetry even, love letters and love talk
breathing a refined, almost chivalric, spirit,—such is

the strange fabric of this drama, at once passionate, derisive, fanfaronading, tragic and burlesque, where the grand style and the most graceful narrative tread on the heels of provincial patois and popular saws. . . .

"Petronius' book belongs essentially to the class of *Satirae Menippeae,* of which Varro had given the first example in the works he composed in imitation of the Greek Menippus, and of which Seneca's *Apocolocyntosis* is another capital instance."

All Critics agree upon the excellence of the *Satyricon* as a work of art, though many take exception to the grossness of the subject matter. Indeed there can be no two opinions as to the brilliancy and refinement of our Author's style generally; while the vivid picturesqueness of the narrative on the one hand, and the perfect adaptation of the language to the rank and idiosyncrasy of the interlocutors on the other, are particularly noteworthy. "The very criticisms which have been launched against Petronius are mingled with admiring panegyric which a due regard for truth has forced from his assailants; and in the mouth of an enemy, praise counts for much more than blame. Even the barbarians and vulgarities of expressions that at times seem to disfigure his style, are in the eyes of Ménage the perfection of art and appropriateness; he puts them only in the mouths of servants and debauchees devoid of any touch of refinement. Note on the other hand with what elegance he makes his well-born characters speak. Petronius assigns to each one of his actors the language most suited to him. This is a merit precious in direct ratio to its rarity; the shadows with which a skillful painter darkens his canvas, only serve to bring out in more startling relief the beauties of the picture. Justus Lipsius epigrammatically styles him *auctor purissimae impuritatis."* (Héguin de Guerle.)

The first thing to strike us is the brilliancy and liveliness of the book,—fragmentary as is the condition in which it has come down to us—as a *Novel of Adventure.* The reader is hurried on, his interest forever on the stretch, from episode to episode of the exciting, and more often than not scandalous, adventures of the disreputable band of light-hearted gentlemen of the road, whose leader is that most audacious and irresponsible of amiable scamps, Encolpius, the narrator of the moving tale. With the exception of the six Chapters devoted to describing the glories and absurdities of Trimalchio's Feast, which form a long episode apart, and a most entertaining one, the action never pauses. From lecture-room to house of ill-fame, from country mansion to country tavern, from the market for stolen goods in a city slum to the Chapel of Priapus, from a harlot's palace to a rich parvenu's table, from Picture Gallery to the public baths, from ship and shipwreck to a luxurious life of imposture in a wealthy provincial town, we are hurried along in breathless haste. The pace is tremendous, but the road bristles with hairbreadth escapes and stirring incidents, and is never for one instant dull or tame. Probably the nearest parallel in other literature is the so-called *Picaresque* romances of Spain, of which Don Pablo de Segovia; Lazarillo de Tormes; and, if we regard it of Spanish origin, the incomparable Gil Blas de Santillana, may be taken as typical examples.

A mere Novel of Adventure then? Not so! The *Satyricon* is this; but it is a great deal besides. It abounds in clear-sighted and instructive *apercus* on education, literature and art, and contemporary deficiencies in these domains; its prose is interspersed with many brilliant fragments of verse, mostly parodies and burlesques, some ludicrous, some beautiful. Over and above its merits as a tale, it is a copious literary miscellany, overflowing with wit and wisdom, drollery and sarcasm.

Last but not least, his work of fine, if irregular, genius contains probably the most lifelike and discriminating character painting in the realm of every-day life to be found in all the range of Ancient literature. To appreciate this, it is only necessary to name three or four of the principal dramatis personæ:—

Encolpius, the gay, unprincipled profligate, but never altogether worthless, narrator of the story;

Ascyltos, his comrade and rival, as immoral and good for nothing as the other, but without his redeeming touch of gentlemanliness and "honour among thieves";

Giton, the minion, changeable and capricious, with his pretty face and wheedling ways;

Tryphaena, the beautiful wanton, who "travels the world for her pleasures";

Lichas, the overbearing and vindictive merchant and Sea-captain; Quartilla, the lascivious and unscrupulous votary of Priapus; Circe, the lovely "femme incomprise" of Croton; and finally, the never to be for-

gotten Eumolpus, the mad poet, the disreputable and
starving pedant, at once "childlike and bland" with an
ineffable naivete of simple conceit, and frankly given
up to the pursuit of the most abominable immoralities,
now bolting from the shower of stones his ineradi-
cable propensity for reciting his own poetry has pro-
voked, now composing immortal verse, calm amid the
horrors of storm and wreck and utterly oblivious of
impending death.

Another point, the admirably clever adaptation of
the language to the social position and character of the
persons speaking, merits a word or two more. While
both the general narrative, and the conversation of the
educated dramatis personæ, Eumolpus for instance,
are marked by a high degree of correctness of diction
and elegance of phrase, the talk of such characters as
Trimalchio and his freedmen friends, Habinnas and
the rest, and other uneducated or half-educated persons, is full not merely of vulgarisms and popular
words, but of positive blunders and downright bad
grammar. These mistakes of course are intentional,
and it is only another proof of the lack of humour and
want of common sense that often marked the indus-
trious and meritorious scholars, particularly German
scholars, of the old school, that some Commentators
have actually gone out of their way to correct these
errors in the text of Petronius. There are hundreds
of them; two or three examples must suffice here.
Libra rubricata says Trimalchio (Ch. VII.—xlvi),
meaning *libros rubricatos*. "lawbooks," and *vetuo* "I
forbid," while his guests indulge in such glaring sole-

cisms as *malus fatus, exhortavit, naufragarunt.* The whole of Chapter VII., where Trimalchio's guests converse freely with one another in the temporary absence of their host, and afterwards Trimalchio harangues the company on various subjects, is full of these diverting "howlers."

From the Philologist's point of view the book is particularly valuable as containing almost our only specimens of the Roman popular, country speech,— the *lingua Romana rusticana,* so all important as the link between literary Latin and the Romance languages of modern Europe. Two or three examples again must suffice: *minutus populus,* exactly the modern French "le menu peuple," *urceatim plovebat,* "it rained in bucketfuls," *non est miscix,* "he's no shirker," *bono fili est,* "he has good stuff in him." It is also a storehouse of popular saws and sayings, sometimes of a fine, vigorous outspokenness, not to say coarseness of expression, such as: *caldum meiiere et frigidum potare,* "to piss hot and drink cold," *sudor per bifurcam volabat,* "the sweat was pouring down between my legs," *lassus tanquam caballus in clivo,* "as tired as a carthorse at a hill."

"In addition to the corruptions in the text," Prof. Ramsay writes in the "Dictionary of Greek and Roman Biography," (Art. "Petronius" p. 217), "which are so numerous and hopeless as to render whole sentences unintelligible, there are doubtless a multitude of strange words and of phrases not elsewhere to be found; but this circumstance need excite no surprise when we remember the various topics which fall under discussion, and the singular personages grouped together on the scene. The most remarkable and startling peculiarities may be considered as the phraseology appropriate to the characters by whom they are uttered, the language of ordinary conversation, the familiar slang in every-day use among the hybrid population of Campania, closely resembling in all probability the dialect of the Atellan farces. On the other hand, wherever the author may be supposed to be speaking in his own person, we are deeply impressed by the extreme felicity of the style, which, far from bearing marks of decrepitude or decay, is redolent of spirit, elasticity, and vigorous freshness."

As to the text, the following paragraphs from Prof. Ramsay's article (Dict. of Greek and Roman Biography, Art. "Petronius," p. 118) give a complete statement which it is impossible to improve upon. "Many attempts," he writes, "have been made to account for the strangely mutilated condition in which the piece has been transmitted to modern times. It has been suggested by some that the blanks were caused by the scruples of pious transcribers, who omitted those parts which were most licentious; while others have not hesitated to declare their conviction that the worst passages were studiously selected. Without meaning to advocate this last hypothesis—and we can scarcely believe that Burmann was in earnest when he propounded it—it is clear that the first explanation is altogether unsatisfactory, for it appears to be impossible that what was passed over could have been more offensive than much of what was retained. According to another theory, what we now possess must be re-garded as striking and favourite extracts, copied out into the common-place book of some scholar in the Middle Ages; a supposition applicable to the Supper of Trimalchio and the longer poetical essays, but which fails for the numerous short and abrupt fragments breaking off in the middle of a sentence. The most simple solution of the difficulty seems to be the true one. The existing MMS. proceeded, in all likelihood, from two or three archetypes, which may have been so much damaged by neglect that large portions were rendered illegible, while whole leaves and sections may have been torn out or otherwise destroyed.

"The Editio Princeps of the fragments of Petronius was printed at Venice by Bernardinus de Vitalibus, 4to. 1499; and the second at Leipzig, by Jacobus Thanner, in 1500; but these editions, and those which followed for upwards of a hundred and fifty years, exhibited much less than we now possess. For, about the middle of the seventeenth century, an individual who assumed the designation of Martinus Statilius, although his real name was Petrus Petitus, found a MS. at Traun in Dalmatia, containing nearly entire the Supper of Trimalchio, which was wanting in all former copies. This was published separately at Padua, in a very incorrect state (8vo. 1664), without the knowl-edge of the discoverer, again by Petitus himself (8vo. Paris, 1664), and immediately gave rise to a fierce controversy, in which the most learned men of that day took a share, one party receiving it without suspicion as a genuine relic of antiquity, while their opponents with great vehemence contended that it was spurious. The strife was not quelled until the year 1669, when the MS. was despatched from the Library of the proprietor, Nicolaus Cippius, at Traun, to Rome, where, having been narrowly scrutinized by the most competent judges, it was finally pronounced to be at least three hundred years old, and, since no forgery of such a nature could have been executed at that epoch, the sceptics were compelled reluctantly to admit that their doubts were ill founded. The title of the Codex, commonly known as the *Codex Traguriensis,* was *Petronii Arbitri Satyri Fragmenta ex libro quinto decimo et sexto decimo,* and then follow the words 'Num alio genere furiarum,' etc.

"Stimulated, it would appear, by the interest excited during the progress of this discussion, and by the favour with which the new acquisition was now universally regarded, a certain Francis Nodot published at Rotterdam (12mo. 1693) what professed to be the Satyricon of Petronius complete, taken, it was said, from a MS. found at Belgrade, when that city was captured in 1688, a MS. which Nodot declared had been presented to him by a Frenchman high in the Imperial service. The fate of this volume was soon decided. The imposture was so palpable that few could be found to advocate the pretensions put forth on its behalf, and it was soon given up by all. It is sometimes, however, printed, along with the genuine text, but in a different type, so as to prevent the possibility of mistake. Besides this, a pretended fragment, said to have been obtained from the monastery of St. Gall, was printed

in 1800, with notes and a French translation by Lalle-
mand, but it seems to have deceived nobody."

In the present version the portions of the narrative
derived from this alleged Belgrade MS. are not specially distinguished from the genuine text; this is done
advisedly, in order not to interrupt the continuity of
the story. This does not of course for a moment
imply that these interpolations are regarded as other
than spurious, but as they are both amusing reading
in themselves as well as admirable imitations of our
Author's style, and supply obvious lacunæ in the plot,
making the whole book more interesting and coherent,
they have been retained as an integral part of the work.
The critical reader can at once detect these passages
by a reference to the "Synopsis of the Plot," given on
p. LXIII below, where they are duly marked off. The
short (and highly diverting) episode contained in the
St. Gall forgery (end of Chapter IV.) has also been
retained, but is included within square brackets, to
distinguish it from the genuine text.

We append three or four extracts bearing upon
Petronius and the Satyricon, and interesting either on
account of the source from which they come, the
quaintness of their expression, or the weight of their
authority.

From the "Age of Petronius," by Ch. Beck (Vol. VI.
of Memoirs of the American Academy of Arts and
Sciences, New Series, 4to. Cambridge, U. S. A., 1856):

"Among the small number of Latin writers of prose
fiction, Petronius, the author of the *Satyricon*, occupies
a prominent place. . . . As to this book, the quality

of its language and style and the nature of its contents constitute it one of the most interesting and important relics of Roman literature, antiquities and history.

"The work, at least the portion which has come down to us, contains the adventures of a dissipated, unprincipled, but clever, cultivated and well informed young man, Encolpius, the hero himself being the narrator. The book opens with a discussion on the defects of the existing system of education, in which the shortcomings of both teachers and parents are pointed out. Next follows a scene in the Forum, in which the hero and his companion, Ascyltos, are concerned, and which exhibits some of the abuses connected with judicial proceedings. After a brief and passing mention of the vices and hypocrisy of the priests, the highly interesting portion containing an account of the banquet of Trimalchio follows. This is succeeded by the account of the acquaintance which the hero, disappointed and dispirited by the faithless conduct of his companion, forms with a philosopher, Eumolpus, who besides discussing some subjects relating to art, especially painting, and to literature, gives an account of his infamous proceedings in corrupting the son of a family in whose house he had been hospitably received. The hero accepts the invitation of the philosopher to accompany him on an excursion to Tarentum. The account of the voyage, of the discovery made by Encolpius that he is on board a vessel owned by a person whose vengeance he had just ground to apprehend, of his fruitless attempt to escape detection, of the reconciliation of the hostile parties, and of the destruction of the vessel and the greater portion of the passengers by shipwreck, is full of interest. The hero and his immediate companions, being the only persons that escaped death, make their way to Croton, where Eumolpus, by representing himself as the owner of valuable and extensive possessions in Africa, works so upon the avarice and cupidity of the inhabitants, who are described as a set of legacy-hunters by profession, that he meets with the most hospitable reception. An intrigue of the hero with a beautiful lady of the city occupies a large part of this section of the story. The book closes with an account of the measures which Eumolpus takes for the purpose of avoiding the detection of his fraud, by working anew upon the avarice of his hosts. The close is abrupt as the beginning had been; the book is incomplete in both parts; the end, as well as the beginning, is wanting.

"That the author of this work was a man of genius is unquestionable. The narrative of the events of the story is simple,—exciting, without exhausting, the interest of the reader, the description of customs, chiefly those of the middle classes of society, is invaluable to the antiquarian, and the importance of the work in this respect can scarcely be overrated; the personages introduced into the story are drawn with such a clearness of perception of their characteristics, and such an accuracy of portraiture, extending to the very peculiarities of the language used by each, that they appear to live and breathe and move before our eyes."

From Dunlop's History of Fiction ("The History

of Fiction"; by John Dunlop, 4th ed. 1876): "The most celebrated fable of ancient Rome is the work of Petronius Arbiter, perhaps the most remarkable fiction which has dishonoured the literature of any nation. It is the only fable of that period now extant, but is a strong proof of the monstrous corruption of the times in which such a production could be tolerated, though no doubt writings of bad moral tendency might be circulated before the invention of printing, without arguing the depravity they would have evinced, if presented to the world subsequent to that period.

"The work of Petronius is in the form of a satire, and, according to some commentators, is directed against the vices of the court of Nero, who is thought to be delineated under the names of Trimalchio and Agamemnon,—an opinion which has been justly ridiculed by Voltaire. The satire is written in a manner which was first introduced by Varro; verses are intermixed with prose, and jests with serious remarks. It has much of the air of a romance, both in the incidents and their disposition; but the story is too well known, and too scandalous, to be particularly detailed.

"The scene is laid in Magna Graecia; Encolpius is the chief character in the work, and the narrator of events;—he commences by a lamentation on the decline of eloquence, and while listening to the reply of Agamemnon, a professor of oratory, he loses his companion, Ascyltos. Wandering through the town in search of him, he is finally conducted by an old woman to a retirement where the incidents that occur are analogous to the scene. The subsequent adventures,—

the feast of Trimalchio,—the defection and return of
Giton,—the amour of Eumolpus in Bithynia,—the
voyaging in the vessel of Lichas,—the passion and disappointment of Circe, follow each other without much
art of arrangement, an apparent defect which may
arise from the mutilated form in which the satire has
descended to us.

"The style of Petronius has been much applauded
for its elegance,—it certainly possesses considerable
naivete and grace, and is by much too fine a veil for so
deformed a body."

From Addison's Preface to his Translation of Petronius ("Works of Petronius Arbiter, translated from
the original Latyn by Mr. Addison." 12mo. London
1736):—

" 'Petronius,' says that judicious Critic, Mons. St.
Evremond, 'is to be admired throughout, for the purity
of his style and the delicacy of his sentiments; but that
which more surprises me, is his great easiness in giving
us ingenuously all sorts of Characters. Terence is
perhaps the only author of Antiquity that enters best
into the nature of persons. But still this fault I find
in him, that he has too little variety; his whole talent
being confined in making servants and old men, a
covetous father and a debauched son, a slave and an
intriguer, to speak properly, according to their several
characters. So far, and no farther, the capacity of
Terence reaches. You must not expect from him
either gallantry or passion, either thoughts or the
discourse of a gentleman. Petronius, who had an universal wit, hits upon the genius of all professions, and

adapts himself, as he pleases, to a thousand different
natures. If he introduces a Declaimer, he assumes his
air and his style so well, that one could say he had
used to declaim all his life. Nothing expresses more
naturally the disorders of a debauched life than the
quarrels of Encolpius and Ascyltos about Giton.

"Is not Quartilla an admirable portrait of a prostitute woman? Does not the marriage of young Giton
and innocent Pannychis give us the image of a complete wantonness?

"All that a sot ridiculously magnificent in banquets,
a vain affecter of niceness, and an impertinent, are able
to do, you have at the Feast of Trimalchio.

"Eumolpus shows us Nero's extravagant folly for
the Theatre, and his vanity in reciting his own poems;
and you may observe, as you run over so many noble
verses, of which he makes an ill use, that an excellent
poet may be a very ill man. . . . The infirmity he has
of making verses out of season, even at death's door;
his fluentness in repeating his compositions in all places
and at all times, answers his ridiculous setting out,
where he tells him, 'I am a Poet, and as I hope, of no
ordinary genius'. . . .

"There is nothing so natural as the character of
Chrysis, and none of our confidantes come near her.
Not to mention her first conversation with Polyaenus,
—what she tells him of her mistress, upon the affront
she received, has an inimitable simplicity. But nobody,
besides Petronius, could have described Circe, so
beautiful, so voluptuous, and so polite. Enothea, the
Priestess of Priapus, ravishes me with the miracles

she promises, with her enchantments, her sacrifices, her sorrow for the death of the consecrated goose, and the manner in which she is pacified when Polyaneus makes her a present, with which she might purchase a goose and the gods too, if she thought fit.

"Philumena, that complaisant lady, is no less entertaining, who after she had cullied several men out of their estates, in the flower of her beauty, now being old and by consequence unfit for pleasures, endeavored to keep up this noble trade by the means of her children, whom she introduced with a thousand fine discourses to old men, who had no heirs of their own.

"In a word, there is no part of Nature, no profession, which Petronius doth not admirably paint. He is a Poet, an Orator, and a Philosopher, at his pleasure."

Lastly Teufel, writing of the *Satyricon* in Pauly's *Encyclopædia* (Vol. V., p. 1404), says:

"The whole plan of the work is that of a novel; two freedmen, Encolpius and Acyltos, are enamoured of a boy Giton, and the adventures which have their origin in this circumstance, and which they encounter severally, the acquaintances which they make (for instance of Trimalchio and Eumolpus), form the contents at least of that portion of the book which has come down to us. But the book contains in this dress of a narrative, descriptions of manners, partly of single places (for example of Croton), partly of certain classes (for example of Trimalchio, a rich upstart, who apes the manners of a refined man of the world, but exposes himself most ridiculously, of Encolpius, a good-natured, cowardly and licentious Greek, of Eumolpus,

a vain and tasteless poet, and at the same time a
thoroughly demoralized preacher of virtue), all drawn
with masterly truthfulness even to the minutest detail.
The tone is throughout humorous; the *dramatis personæ* act and speak, even in the most offensive circumstances, with an openness, unconcern and self-satisfac-
tion, as if they had the most undoubted right to be and
think as they do; at the same time, a vein of gentle
irony pervades the whole, which indicates the author's
moral independence and higher standpoint, as well as
his sincere gratification at the amusing and filthy scenes
which he describes; he accompanies his heroes at every
step with a smile on his lips and a low laugh.   The
work belongs therefore, by its contents as well as its
tone, to the department of satire, resembling in tone
Horace, in form the Menippean satire.   For not only
does the language occasionally pass over from prose to
verse (limping iambs and trochees), but entire poems
of greater extent are interwoven (*Troiae Halosis* and
Bellum Civile), which are usually put in the mouth of
Eumolpus, and which always have a satirical object,
sometimes a double one, as in the case with the *Bellum
Civile*, which ridicules Lucan, as well as his opponents
personified by Eumolpus, the writer with genuine
humour placing himself above both, and dealing
against both his blows with impartial justice.   The
language is always suited to the character of the
persons speaking, elegant in Encolpius, bombastic in
Trimalchio.   The language put in the mouth of the
last is for us an invaluable specimen of the *lingua
Romana rustica,* as it obtained in that part of Italy

where the scene is laid,—in Campania, and especially Naples. In conformity with the originally Greek character of this region, the language of Trimalchio and his companions is full of Greek words and Grecisms of the boldest kind (such as coupling the neuter plural with the verb in the singular, as in LXXI.). Characteristic of the local dialect are the many archaisms, compounds not known in the written language, the frequent solecisms, the many proverbial and extravagant expressions, the numerous oaths and curses."

A brilliant passage from Emile Thomas' remarkable study of Petronius and contemporary Roman society, entitled, "Petrone: L'Envers de la Société Romaine" (Paris 1902), may fitly sum up the situation. "This romance," he writes, "such delightful and at the same time such difficult reading, a work at once exquisite and repulsive, gives us by virtue of its defects no less than of its merits a fairly adequate representation of the *under-side* of Roman civilization. Would it not be a gain, and a great one, for the systematic history of morals and literature at Rome to restore this work to its proper place? and is not this place pretty well identical, barring of course the difference of field and form, with that reserved in Greek Art for the vases, statuettes and pottery of Tanagra, and of the periods before and after Tanagra, in one word, whatever allows us to comprehend, or at least get a glimpse of, the Ancient world under the aspects of its everyday life? Everybody knows how successful has been the revolution, and how fruitful in results that has been brought about under our own eyes in this department of Greek Archæology.

"Well! here (in Petronius) we have among the authors of Rome a veritable *genre* painter, of a sort to take the place for us, at any rate in part, of the graceful vase-paintings of Antiquity, as well as of the grotesques of Greek art.

"From yet another aspect, not a few points of resemblance may be detected between Petronius and the lighter literary productions, novels, tales, burlesque narratives, *vers de societe,* and even journals, of the last two Centuries. Our Author is refined, not to say *blasé,* but none the less inquisitive, full both of sagacity and passion, always exact, and above and beyond all else, a supreme master of style. Laying aside all false delicacy, let us hear what he has to tell us of the daily routine, of the outward aspect, and even of the hidden secrets, of Roman existence. Nowhere else has human life been lived on an ampler scale; no other people, no other society, has ever displayed so much variety, so many contrasts, such heights of grandeur and such depths of degradation."

CHAPTER ONE

SUCH a long time has passed since first I promised you the story of my adventures I am resolved to keep my word to-day, seeing we are here happily met together to season those matters of learning that form our serious business with lively conversation and tales of a merry and diverting sort. Fabricius Veiento was discoursing very wisely to us just now on the follies of superstition, exposing the various forms of priestly charlatantry, the holy men's mania for prophecy, and the effrontery they display in expounding mysteries they very often utterly fail to comprehend themselves. Is it not much the same type of madness that afflicts our declaimers, who shout: "These wounds I got, defending our common liberties; this eye I lost in your behalf. Give me a helping hand to lead me to my children, for my poor maimed limbs refuse to bear my weight." Even such extravagances might be borne, if they really served to guide beginners in the way of eloquence; but all pupils gain by these high-flown themes, these empty sounding phrases, is this, that on entering the forum they imagine themselves transported into a new and strange world. This is the reason, in my opinion, why young men grow up such blockheads in the schools, because they neither see nor hear one single thing connected with the usual cir-

cumstances of everyday life, nothing but stuff about
pirates lurking on the seashore with fetters in their
hands, tyrants issuing edicts to compel sons to cut off
their own fathers' heads, oracles in times of pestilence
commanding three virgins or more to be sacrificed to
stay the plague,—honey-sweet, well-rounded sentences, words and facts alike as it were, besprinkled
with poppy and sesame.

Under such a training it is no more possible to ac-
quire good taste than it is not to stink, if you live in
a kitchen. Give me leave to tell you that you rhetori-
cians are chiefly to blame for the ruin of Oratory, for
with your silly, idle phrases, meant only to tickle the
ears of an audience, you have enervated and deboshed
the very substance of true eloquence.

Young men were not bound down to declamations
in the days when Sophocles and Euripides found the
very words they wanted to best express their meaning.
No cloistered professor had as yet darkened men's in-
tellects, when Pindar and the nine Lyric bards shrank
from emulating the Homeric note. And not to cite
poets exclusively,—I cannot see that either Plato or
Demosthenes ever practised this sort of mental exercise. A noble, and so to say chaste, style is not over-
loaded with ornament, not turgid; its own natural
beauty gives it elevation.

Then after a while this windy, extravagant deluge
of words invaded Athens from Asia, and like a malig-
nant star, blasting the minds of young men aiming at
lofty ideals, instantly broke up all rules of art and
struck eloquence dumb. Since that day who has

reached the perfection of Thucydides, the glory of Hyperides? Nay! not a poem has been written of bright and wholesome complexion; but all, as if fed on the same unhealthy diet, have lacked stamina to attain old age. Painting moreover shared the same fate, after Egypt presumptuously invented a compendious method for that noble Art.

Such and suchlike reflections I was indulging in one day before a numerous audience, when Agamemnon came up, curious to see who it was they were listening to so attentively. Well! he declined to allow me to declaim longer in the Portico than he had himself sweated in the schools; but "Young man," he cries, "seeing your words are something better than mere popular commonplaces, and—a very rare occurrence —you are an admirer of sound sense, I will confide to you a professional secret. In the choice of these exercises it is not the masters that are to blame. They are forced to be just as mad as all the rest; for if they refuse to teach what pleases their scholars, they will be left, as Cicero says, to lecture to empty benches. Just as false-hearted sycophants, scheming for a seat at a rich man's table, make it their chief business to discover what will be most agreeable hearing to their host, for indeed their only way to gain their end is by cajolment and flattery; so a professor of Rhetoric, unless like a fisherman he arm his hook with the bait he knows the fish will take, may stand long enough on his rock without a chance of success.

"Whose fault is it then? It is the parents deserve censure, who will not give their children the advan-

tages of a strict training. In the first place their hopes,
like everything else, are centred in ambition, and so
being impatient to see their wishes fulfilled, they hurry
lads into the forum when still raw and half taught,
and indue mere babes with the mantle of eloquence, an
art they admit themselves to be equalled by none in
difficulty. If only they would let them advance step
by step in their tasks, so that serious students might be
broken in by solid reading, steady their minds with
the precepts of philosophy, chasten their style with
unsparing correction, study deep and long what they
propose to imitate, and refuse to be dazzled by puerile
graces, then and then only would the grand old type
of Oratory recover its former authority and stateli-
ness. Nowadays, boys waste their time at school; as
youths, they are jeered at in the forum, and what is
worse than either, no one will acknowledge as an old
man the faultiness of the teaching he received in his
younger days.

"But that you may not imagine I disapprove of
satirical impromptus in the Lucilian vein, I will myself throw my notions on this matter into verse:

"He that would be an orator, must strive
  To follow out the discipline of old,
  And heed the laws of stern frugality;
  Not his to haunt the Court with fawning brow,
  Nor sit a flatterer at great folks' boards;
  Not his with boon companions o'er the wine
  To overcloud his brain, nor at the play
  To sit and clap, agape at actors' tricks.
  But whether to Tritonia's famous halls

The Muses lead his steps, or to those walls
That Spartan exiles rear'd or where
The Sirens' song thrill'd the enraptured air
Of all his tasks let Poesy be first,
And Homer's verse the fount to quench his thirst.
Soon will be master deep Socratic lore,
And wield the arms Demosthenes erst bore.
Then to new modes must he in turn be led,
And Grecian wit to Roman accents wed.
Nor in the forum only will he find
Meet occupation for his busy mind;
On books he'll feast, the poet's words of fire,
Heroic tales of War and Tully's patriot ire,
Such be thy studies; then, whate'er the theme,
Pour forth thine eloquence in copious stream."

Listening attentively to the speaker, I never noticed
that Ascyltos had given me the slip; and I was still
walking up and down in the gardens full of the burning words I had heard, when a great mob of students
rushed into the Portico. Apparently these had just
come from hearing an impromptu lecture of some critic
or other who had been cutting up Agamemnon's
speech. So whilst the lads were making fun of his
sentiments and abusing the arrangement of the whole
discourse, I seized the opportunity to escape, and
started off at a run in pursuit of Ascyltos. But I was
heedless about the road I followed, and indeed felt by
no means sure of the situation of our inn, the result
being that whichever direction I took, I presently
found myself back again at my starting point. At last,

exhausted with running and dripping with sweat, I came across a little old woman, who was selling herbs.

"Prithee, good mother," say I, "can you tell me where I live?"—Charmed with the quiet absurdity of my question, "Why certainly!" she replied; and getting up, went on before me. I thought she must be a witch; but presently, when we had arrived at a rather shy neighborhood, the obliging old lady drew back the curtain of a doorway, and said, "Here is where you ought to live."

I was just protesting I did not know the house, when I caught sight of mysterious figures prowling between rows of name-boards, and naked harlots. Then when too late, I saw I had been brought into a house of ill fame. So cursing the old woman's falseness, I threw my robe over my head and made a dash right through the brothel to the opposite door, when lo! just on the threshold, whom should I meet but Ascyltos, fagged out and half dead like myself? You would have thought the very same old hag had been his conductress. I made him a mocking bow, and asked him what he was doing in such a disreputable place?

Wiping the sweat from his face with both hands, he replied, "If you only knew what happened to me!"

"Why! what has happened?" said I.

Then in a faint voice he went on, "I was wandering all over the town, without being able to discover where I had left our inn, when a respectable looking man accosted me, and most politely offered to show me the way. Then after traversing some very dark and intricate alleys, he brought me where we are, and producing his affair, began begging me to grant him my favours. In two twos the woman had taken the fee for the room, and the man laid hold of me; and if I had not proved the stronger, I should have fared very ill indeed."

While Ascyltos was thus recounting his adventures, up came his respectable friend again, accompanied by a woman of considerable personal attractions, and addressing himself to Ascyltos, besought him to enter, assuring him he had nothing to fear, and that as he would not consent to play the passive, he should do the active part. The woman on her side was very anxious I should go with her. Accordingly we followed the pair, who led us among the name-boards, where we saw in the chambers persons of both sexes behaving in such fashion I concluded they must every one have been drinking satyrion. On seeing us, they endeavoured to allure us to sodomy with enticing gestures; and suddenly one fellow with his clothes well tucked up assails Ascyltos, and throwing him down on a bed, tries to get to work a-top of him. I sprang to the sufferer's rescue, and uniting our efforts, we make short work of the ruffian. Ascyltos bolts out of the house, and away, leaving me to escape their beastly advances as best I might; but discovering I was too strong for them and in no mood for trifling, they left me alone.

After running about almost over the city, I caught sight of Giton, as it were a fog, standing at the corner of an alley close to the door of our inn, and hurried to join him. I asked my favourite whether he had got anything ready for our dinner, whereupon the lad

sat down on the bed and began wiping away the tears
with his thumb. Much disturbed at my favourite's
distress, I demanded what had happened. For a long
time I could not drag a word out of him,—not indeed
till I had added threats to prayers. Then he reluctantly told me. "That favourite or comrade of yours
came into our lodging just now, and set to work to
force me. When I screamed he drew a sword and
said, 'If you're a Lucretia, you've found a Tarquin'."

Hearing this, I exclaimed, shaking my two fists in
Ascyltos' face. "What have you to say now, you
pathic prostitute, you, whose very breath is abominable?" Ascyltos feigned extreme indignation, and immediately repeated my gesture with greater emphasis,
cried in still louder tones, "Will you hold your tongue,
you filthy gladiator, who after murdering your host,
had luck enough to escape from the criminal's cage at
the Amphitheatre. Will you hold your tongue you
midnight cut-throat, who never, when at your bravest,
durst face an honest woman? Didn't I serve you for a
minion in an orchard, just as this lad does now in an
inn?"

"Did you or did you not," I interrupted, "sneak off
from the master's lecture?"

"What was I to do, fool, when I was dying of hunger? Stop and listen to a string of phrases no better
than the tinkling of broken glass or the nonsensical in-
terpretations in dream books? By great Hercules,
you are dead baser than I; to compass a dinner you
have condescended to flatter a Poet!" This ended our
unseemly wrangle, and we both burst into a fit of

laughter, and proceeded to discuss other matters in a more peaceable tone.

But the recollection of his late violence coming over me afresh, "Ascyltos," I said, "I see we can get on together, so let us divide between us our bits of common funds, and each try to make head against poverty on his own bottom. You are a scholar; so am I. I don't wish to spoil your profits, so I'll take up another line. Else shall we find a thousand causes of quarrel every day, and soon make ourselves the talk of the town."

Ascyltos raised no objections, merely saying, "For to-day, as we have accepted, in our quality of men of letters, an invitation to dine out, don't let us lose our evening; but to-morrow, since you wish it, I will look out for a new lodging and another bedfellow."

"Poor work," said I, "putting off the execution of a good plan." It was really my naughty passions that urged me to so speedy a parting; indeed I had been long wishing to be rid of his jealous observation, in order to renew my old relations with my sweet Giton. Ascyltos, mortally offended at my remark, rushed out of the room without another word. So sudden a departure boded ill; for I knew his ungovernable temper and the strength of his passions. So I went after him, to keep an eye on his doings and guard against their consequences; but he slipped adroitly out of my sight, and I wasted a long time in a fruitless search for the rascal.

After looking through the whole city, I came back to my little room, and now at length claiming my full tale of kisses, I clip my darling lad in the tightest of embraces; my utmost hopes of bliss are fulfilled to the envy of all mankind. The rites were not yet complete, when Ascyltos crept up stealthily to the door, and violently bursting in the bolts, caught me at play with his favourite. His laughter and applause filled the room, and tearing off the mantle that covered us, "Why! what are you after," he cries, "my sainted friend? What! both tucked cosily under one coverlet?" Nor did he stop at words, but detaching the strap from his wallet, he fell to thrashing me with no perfunctory hand, seasoning his blows with insulting remarks,—"This is the way you divide stock with a comrade, is it? Not so fast, my friend." So unexpected was the attack I was obliged to put up with the blows in silence. Accordingly I took the matter as a joke, and it was well I did so; otherwise I should have had to fight my rival. My counterfeited merriment calmed his anger, and he even smiled faintly. "Look you, Encolpius," said he, "are you so buried in your pleasures, you never reflect that our money is exhausted, and the trifles we have left are valueless. Town is good for nothing in the summer days; there'll be better luck in the country. Let's go visit our friends."

CHAPTER TWO

NECESSITY constrained me to approve his advice and restrain the expression of my resentment. So, loading Giton with our scanty baggage, we quitted the city and made our way to the country house of Lycurgus, a Roman knight. Ascyltos had been a minion in former days, so he gave us an excellent reception, and the company assembled there rendered our entertainment still more delightful. First and foremost was Tryphaena, a very handsome woman, who had come with Lychas, master of a ship and owner of estates near the sea-coast.

Words cannot describe the pleasures we enjoyed in this most delightful spot,—though Lycurgus's table was frugal enough. You must know we lost no time in pairing off as lovers. The lovely Tryphaena was my fancy, and readily acceded to my wishes. But scarcely was I in enjoyment of her favours, when Lichas, furious at his lady-love being filched from him, insisted I must indemnify him for the injury done him. She had long been his mistress; so he made the festive proposal that I should make good his loss in person. He pressed me passionately; but Tryphaena possessing my heart, my ears were deaf to his importunities. My refusal made him still more eager and he followed me about like a dog, and actually came into my chamber one night. Finding his entreaties scorned, he tried to force me; but I shouted so loudly I roused the household and my favour of Lycurgus's countenance was saved from the ruffian's attempts.

Eventually thinking Lycurgus's house inconvenient for his purpose, he endeavoured to persuade me to be his guest. When I refused his invitation, he got Tryphaena to use her influence. The latter begged me to comply with Lichas's wishes, what made her so ready to do so being the prospect of leading a more independent life there. Accordingly I follow where my love leads the way. But Lycurgus, having renewed his formed relations with Ascyltos, would not let him go. So we agreed that he should stop with Lycurgus, whilst we accompanied Lichas, resolving at the same time that, as opportunity offered, we should each and all lay hands on anything handy for the common stock.

My consent delighted Lichas beyond measure. He hurried on our departure all he could, and forthwith bidding our friends farewell, we arrived the same day at his house. Lichas had cleverly arranged it in such a way that he sat beside me during the journey, while Tryphaena was next to Giton. This he had contrived because he knew the woman's notorious fickleness, and the result justified his expectations. In fact she instantly fell in love with the lad, as I saw easily enough. Lichas moreover made a point of drawing my attention to the circumstance, and assured me there was no doubt about it. This made me receive his advances more complacently, at which he was overjoyed. He felt certain the injury my mistress was doing me would turn my love into contempt, and that consequently out of pique against Tryphaena, I should be the more disposed to welcome his proposals.

Such was the state of affairs under Lichas's roof. Tryphaena was desperately enamoured of Giton; Giton's whole heart was aflame for Tryphaena, I hated the sight of both; while Lichas, studying to please me, contrived some fresh diversion every day. Doris, his pretty wife, eagerly seconded his efforts, and that so charmingly she soon drove Tryphaena from my heart. A wink informed Doris of the state of my feelings, and she returned the compliment with alluring glances; so that this mute language, anticipating the tongue, furtively expressed the mutual liking we had simultaneously conceived for one another.

I soon saw Lichas was jealous, and this made me cautious; while the quick eyes of love had already revealed to the wife the husband's designs on me. The first opportunity we had of conversing together, she announced her discovery to me. I frankly admitted the fact, and told her how austerely I had always treated his advances. But like a wise, discreet woman, she only said, "Well! well! we must act judiciously in the matter;" I followed her advice, and found that,— To yield to the one was to win the other.

Meanwhile, while Giton was recruiting his exhausted strength, Tryphaena was for returning to me; but on my repulsing her overtures, her love changed into furious hate. Nor was the ardent little wanton long in discovering my dealings both with husband and wife. The former's naughtiness with me she made

light of, for she lost nothing by it; but she went
savagely for Doris and her secret pleasures. She de-
nounced her to Lichas, whose jealousy proving
stronger than his love, he prepares for revenge. However Doris, warned by Tryphaena's maid to look out
for storms, refrained from any clandestine meetings
for the present.

When I learned the truth, cursing at once Tryphaena's perfidy and Lichas's ingratitude, I made up
my mind to be gone. Fortune moreover was in my
favour; for the very day before a vessel, dedicated
to Isis and laden with rich offerings for the feast of
the goddess, had run ashore on the rocks of the neighbouring coast.

I talked the matter over with Giton, and he readily
enough agreed to my plan, for Tryphaena, after draining him of his strength, was now openly neglecting
him. Accordingly we set off betimes next day for
the coast, and easily got aboard the wreck from being
known to Lichas's servants, who were in charge. But
finding they insisted on attending us everywhere out
of politeness, so stopping any chance of looting, I left
Giton with them and seizing an opportunity to get
away by myself, crept into the poop, where stood the
image of Isis. This I robbed of a rich mantle and a
silver sistrum, besides appropriating other valuables
from the Captain's cabin. This done, I slipped down
a mooring-rope without anybody seeing me except
Giton, who likewise eluded the men in charge before
very long and sneaked after me.

On his coming up, I showed him my booty, and we

resolved to make the best of our way to Ascyltos, but we could not reach Lycurgus's house till next day. Arrived there, I gave Ascyltos a brief account of the robbery, and of our untoward love adventures. His advice was to get Lycurgus on our side, telling him that fresh persecutions on the part of Lichas had determined our sudden and secret flight. When he heard this Lycurgus took an oath he would never fail us as a bulwark against our enemies.

Our flight was not observed until Tryphaena and Doris awoke and got up; for every morning we made a point of attending these ladies' toilette. Our unwonted absence therefore being noticed, Lichas despatched messengers to look for us, particularly to the sea shore. From them he heard of our having visited the ship, but not a word about the robbery. This was still undiscovered, because the poop lay seawards, and the Master had not as yet returned to his vessel.

Eventually, when no doubt remained as to our flight, which annoyed Lichas extremely, the latter turned furiously upon Doris, considering her to be responsible for it. I will not describe his language nor the violence he indulged in towards her,—indeed I do not know the details. Enough to say that Tryphaena, the originator of all the disturbance, prevailed on Lichas to go and look for us at Lycurgus's house, as being our most likely place of refuge, choosing herself to accompany him thither, that she might find opportunity to load us with the abuse and scorn we had so well merited at her hands.

Setting out next day, they arrived at the mansion.
We were not at home, Lycurgus having taken us to a
feast of Hercules that was being celebrated at a
neighbouring village. Learning this, they followed us
in all haste, and came up with us in the Portico of
the Temple. This appearance disconcerted us not a
little. Lichas instantly began to complain bitterly
of our running away to Lycurgus; but was met with
such an angry brow and haughty air by the latter, that
plucking up a spirit, I loudly cried shame on his
lecherous attempts on my person both under Lycurgus's roof and his own. Tryphaena interfered, but got
the worst of it, too, for I proclaimed her baseness to
the crowds of people our altercation had attracted,
and in token of the truth of my allegations, I showed
them Giton pale and bloodless and myself brought to
death's door by the strumpet's wantonness. The crowd
burst into shouts of laughter, which so abashed our
adversaries that they withdrew, crestfallen and vowing
vengeance.

Perceiving we had quite won Lycurgus over, they
determined to wait for him at his own house, in order
to disabuse his mind of this prepossession in our
favour. The solemnities finished too late for us to
return to the mansion that night; so Lycurgus took
us to a country lodge of his situated half way thither.
Here he left us next morning still asleep, while he
went home himself to attend to the despatch of business. He found Lichas and Tryphaena waiting for
him there, who talked him over so cleverly, they
actually persuaded him to deliver us up into their

hands. Lycurgus, a man naturally cruel and treacherous, meditating how best to betray us, urged Lichas
to go for help, while he went himself to the lodge to
secure our capture.

Arrived there, he accosted us with as harsh a mien
as ever Lichas might have been expected to show;
then, wringing his hands, he upbraided us with our
falsehood to Lichas, and ordered us to be kept fast
prisoners in the chamber where we lay, excluding
Ascyltos and refusing to hear a word from him in our
defence. Taking the latter with him to his mansion, he
left us behind in custody till his return.

On the journey Ascyltos tried in vain to modify
Lycurgus's determination, but neither prayers, caresses
nor tears would move him. Accordingly our comrade
conceived the idea of setting us at liberty by other
means. Indignant at Lycurgus's harshness, he positively refused to sleep with him, and so found himself
in a better position to carry out the plan he had formed.

Waiting till the household were buried in their first
sleep, he took our bits of baggage on his shoulders,
and slipping through a breach in the wall he had pre-
viously marked, he reached the lodge at daybreak.
Entering the house unopposed, he sought our room,
which the guards had taken care to secure. There was
little difficulty in opening the door, for the bolt being
of wood, he loosened this by inserting an iron bar.
Presently the lock dropped off, and awoke us in falling, for we were snoring away in spite of our unhappy
situation. Yet so sound asleep were our guards, being

tired out with watching, that the crash roused no one but ourselves.

Then Ascyltos, entering our prison, briefly told us what he had done for us, nor indeed were many words necessary. While we were busy dressing, it occurred to me to kill the watchman and loot the house. I confided my notion to Ascyltos, who approved of the robbery, but said we could gain our ends better without bloodshed. Accordingly, knowing as he did all the ins and outs of the premises, he led us to the store chamber, the doors of which he undid. Appropriating the more valuable of the contents, we made off while it was still early morning, and avoiding the public roads, never stopped till we deemed ourselves safe from pursuit.

Hereupon Ascyltos, taking breath, declared emphatically what delight he had felt in pillaging Lycurgus's house. He was an arrant miser, he said, and had given him good reason to complain; while he had never paid him a farthing for his nights' work, he had at the same time kept him on very short commons and the thinnest of drink. So niggardly indeed was the fellow that notwithstanding his boundless wealth, he used to deny himself the barest necessities of life.

> Unhappy Tantalus, with plenty curst,
> 'Mid fruits for hunger faints, 'mid streams for
>   thirst:
> The Miser's emblem! who of all possess'd,
> Yet fears to taste, in blessings most unbless'd.

Ascyltos was for returning to Naples that same day.
"But surely," said I, "it is acting imprudently to go to
the very place of all others where they are most likely
to look for us. Let us keep away for a while and
ramble about the country. We have the means to do
it in comfort." My advice was approved, and we set
out for a hamlet embellished with a number of agreeable country residences, where several of our familiars
were enjoying the pleasures of the season. But
scarcely had we covered half the distance when a
storm of rain coming down in bucketfuls compelled
us to fly for shelter to the nearest village. Entering
the inn, we found a crowd of other travellers who had
turned in there to escape the inclemency of the
weather.

The throng prevented our attracting notice, which
made it all the easier for us to pry about in search of
anything we could appropriate. Ascyltos picked up
from the floor, quite unobserved, a little bag containing a number of gold pieces. We were delighted at
this lucky beginning; but fearing some one might claim
the money, we stole away by the back-door. There we
found a servant saddling some horses, who at that
moment left them to go back to the house for something he had forgotten. Profiting by his absence, I
snatched a superb riding-cloak from a saddle, undoing
the straps that fastened it. This done, we made off
into the nearest wood under cover of some outhouses.

Sitting down in the depths of the wood, where we
were in comparative safety, we held a council of war
about concealing the gold, not wishing either to be

accused of the theft or to be robbed of it ourselves. Finally we decided to sew it up in a hem of an old threadbare tunic, which I threw round my shoulders, and entrusted the cloak to Ascyltos, we prepared to start for the city by way of bypaths. But just as we were quitting the forest, we heard a voice pronounce these terrible words: "They shan't escape. They're gone into the wood; and if we spread out and search everywhere, they'll easily be caught."

These words filled us with such consternation that Ascyltos and Giton dashed away through the bushes in the direction of the city; while I stepped back so hurriedly that, without my knowing it, the precious tunic slipped from my shoulders. At length, tired out and unable to go a step further, I lay down under a tree, and then for the first time discovered my loss. Vexation gave me new strength, and starting up again to look for the treasure, I wandered up and down for a long tme in vain, till worn out with toil and trouble I plunged into the darkest recesses of the forest, where I remained for four weary hours. Sick at last of the horrible solitude, I sought a way out, but as I advanced I caught sight of a peasant. Then indeed I wanted all my assurance, and it did not fail me; going boldly up to him, I asked my way to the city, complaining I had been lost for ever so long in the wood. He led me very civilly into the high road, where he came upon two of his comrades, who reported they had searched all the paths through the forest, but had found nothing except a tunic which they show him.

I had not the impudence to claim the garment, as

may be supposed. My vexation redoubled, and I uttered many a groan over my lost gold.

Thus it was already late when I reached the city. Entering the inn, I found Ascyltos stretched half dead on a bed. Disturbed at not seeing the tunic entrusted to my care, Ascyltos eagerly demanded it. After a while my strength came back a little, and I then told him the whole misadventure; but he thought I was joking, and though an appealing flood of tears further confirmed my asseverations, he remained obviously incredulous, thinking I wanted to cheat him out of the money. But after all, what most troubled our minds was the hue and cry after us. I mentioned this to Ascyltos, but he made light of it, having managed to extricate himself successfully from the affair. Besides he was convinced we were safe enough, for we were not known, and nobody had set eyes on us. Still we thought it advisable to feign sickness, so as to have a pretext for keeping our room the longer. But our cash running short, we had to go abroad sooner than we had intended, and under the spur of necessity to sell some of our plunder.

CHAPTER THREE

On the approach of night we took our way to the market-place, where we saw an abundance of goods for sale, not indeed articles of any great value, but rather such as needed the kindly veil of darkness, considering their rather shady origin. Thither we also conveyed our stolen riding-cloak, and seizing the opportunity, displayed a corner of it in a quiet spot, hoping a buyer might be attracted by the beauty of the garment.

It was not long before a countryman, whose face seemed somehow familiar to me, approached in company with a young woman, and began to examine the cloak minutely. On the other part Ascyltos, casting his eye on the rustic customer's shoulders, was instantly struck dumb with surprise. Nor could I myself avoid some perturbation of mind when I saw him; for he appeared to be the identical peasant who had found our old tunic in the loneliness of the wood. Yes! he was the very man. But Ascyltos, afraid to trust his eyes and anxious not to do anything rash, first went up to the fellow as a would-be purchaser, drew the tunic from his shoulders and began to scrutinize it carefully.

By a wonderful stroke of luck the rustic had not as yet had the curiosity to search the seams, but was

offering the thing for sale with an indifferent air as
some beggar-man's leavings. When Ascyltos saw our
money was intact and that the vendor was a person of
no great account, he drew me a little aside from the
throng and said, "Do you observe, comrade, our treasure that I was regretting as lost is come back again?
(That is our tunic and it seems to have the gold pieces
in it still: they haven't been touched. But what can
we do about it? How are we to prove our property?)"
I was greatly cheered not only at beholding our loot
once more, but also because I thus found myself freed
from a villainous suspicion, and at once declared
against any sort of beating about the bush. I advised
we should bring a civil action right out to compel him
to give up the property to its rightful owners by law,
if he refused to do so otherwise.

Not so Ascyltos, who had a wholesome fear of the
law. "Who knows us," he said, "in this place, or will
believe what we say? My own strong opinion is we
should buy the property, our own though it be, now
we see it, and rather pay a small sum to recover our
treasure than get mixed up in a law-suit, the issue of
which is uncertain."

> What worth our laws, when pelf alone is king,
> When to be poor is to be always wrong?
> The Cynic sage himself, stern moralist,
> Is not averse to sell his words for gold;
> Justice is bought, the highest bidder wins,
> A partial Judge directs a venal Court.

But alas! except for a brace of copper coins, which we had purposed to spend on lupins and pease, we were penniless just then. So, for fear the prey might escape us meanwhile, we resolved to part with the cloak at a lower price, making the profit on the one transaction balance the loss on the other. Accordingly we spread out our merchandise; but the woman who had hitherto been standing beside the countryman closely muffled, now suddenly, after carefully scanning certain marks on the cloak, laid hold of the hem with both hands, and screamed out "Stop thieves! Stop thieves!" at the top of her voice.

At this we were not a little disconcerted but that we might not seem to acquiesce without a protest, we in our turn seized the tattered, filthy tunic, and declared no less spitefully it was our goods they had in their possession. But our case was far from being on all fours with theirs; and the crowd, that had gathered at the outcry, began to make fun of our impertinent claim, and not unnaturally, when on the one side they asserted their right to a most valuable cloak, but we to this old rag hardly worth mending. However Ascyltos adroitly stopped their ridicule by crying out, directly he could get a hearing, "Well! look you, every man likes his own property best; let 'em give us up our tunic, and they shall have their cloak."

Both the rustic and the young woman were ready enough to make the exchange; but a couple of attorneys, or to give them their true name night-prowlers, who wanted to appropriate the cloak themselves, demanded that both the articles in dispute should be deposited with them, and the Judge look into the case in the morning; for not only must the ownership of these be investigated, but quite another question altogether as well, to wit, a suspicion of theft on the part of both parties.

The by-standers were by this time all in favour of sequestration, and an individual in the crowd, a bald man with a very pimply face, who was in the habit of undertaking occasional jobs for the lawyers, impounded the cloak, saying he would produce it on the morrow. But the real object was self-evident, that the knavish crew having once got hold of the article in question, they might smuggle it out of the way, while we should be scared by the fear of a charge of theft from putting in an appearance at the appointed time. This was very much what we wanted ourselves, and luck seconded the wishes of both parties. For the countryman, indignant at our requiring the surrender of an old rag, threw the tunic in Ascyltos's face, and withdrawing his own claim altogether, merely demanded the sequestration of the cloak as the only object of litigation. Having thus recovered our treasure, as we felt, we rush off full speed for our inn, and bolting the room door, start making merry over the astuteness both of our opponents and of the crowd, who had exercised so much ingenuity in giving us back our money!

As we were unstitching the tunic to take out the gold pieces, we overheard some one asking the inn-keeper what kind of people they were who had just entered his house. Terrified at the question, I went down after he had gone, to see what was the matter, and found that a Praetor's lictor, whose duty it was to see the names of strangers entered in the public registers, had seen two such enter the inn, whose names he had not yet taken down, and was therefore making inquiries as to their nationality and business. This information the inn-keeper gave in such an off-hand manner as made me suspect his house was not altogether a safe place for us; so, to avoid the chance of arrest, we determined to leave the place and not return till after dark. Accordingly we sallied forth, leaving the care of providing our dinner to Giton.

As our wish was to avoid the frequented streets, we went by way of the more lonely districts of the city. Towards nightfall we met in a remote spot two respectable robed and goodlooking women, and followed them slowly and softly to a small temple, which they entered, and from which a strange humming was audible, like the sound of voices issuing from the recesses of a cavern. Curiosity impelled us likewise to enter the temple, and there we beheld a number of women, resembling Bacchantes, each brandishing an emblem of Priapus in her right hand. This was all we were permitted to see; for the instant they caught sight of us, they set up such a shouting the vault of the sacred building trembled, and tried to seize hold of us. But we fled as fast as our legs would carry us back to our inn.

Scarcely had we eaten our fill of the dinner Giton had provided us, when the door resounded with a most imperative knocking. Turning pale, we de-

manded, "Who's there?"—"Open the door," was the
answer, "and you'll find out." We were still arguing when the bolt tumbled off of itself, the door flew
open and admitted our visitor. This was a woman
with her head muffled, the very same who a little before
had been standing by the countryman's side in the
market. "Ah, ha!" she cried, "did you suppose you
had really made a fool of me? I am Quartilla's maid,
—Quartilla whose devotions before the grotto you disturbed. She is coming in person to the inn, and begs
to speak with you. Do not be afraid; she brings no
accusation, and has no wish to punish your fault. She
only wonders what god it was brought such genteel
young men into her district."

We were still dumb, not knowing in the least what
kind of response to give, when the mistress herself
entered, accompanied only by a young girl, and sitting
down on my couch, wept for ever so long. Not even
then had we a word to offer, but looked on in amazement at this tearful display of pretended grief. When
the enticing shower had exhausted itself, she drew
back the hood that concealed her haughty features,
and wringing her hands till the finger joints cracked,
"What means this recklessness?" she cried; "wherever
have you learned these knavish tricks that for audacity
outdo the heroes of the story-books? By heaven! I
pity you! for be sure no man ever looked with impunity on forbidden sights. Truly our neighbourhood
is so well stocked with deities to hand, you will easier
meet with a god than a man. But don't imagine I've
come here vindictively; I'm more moved by your youth

than angered by the wrong you have done me. It was in sheer ignorance, I still think, you committed your unpardonable act of sacrilege.

"Last night I was grievously tormented, and shaken with such alarming tremblings, I dreaded an attack of tertian ague. So in my sleep I prayed for a remedy, and was bidden seek you out, that you might assuage the violence of the complaint by means of a cunning contrivance also indicated in my dream. But indeed and indeed it is not so much this cure I am exercised about; what wrings my heart and drives me almost to despair is the dread that in your youthful levity you may reveal what you saw in the shrine of Priapus, and betray the counsels of the gods to the common herd. This is why I stretch forth suppliant hands to your knees, and beg and pray you not to turn into ribaldry and jest our nocturnal rites, nor willingly divulge the secrets of so many years,—secrets known to barely a thousand persons all told."

After this impassioned appeal she again burst into tears, and shaken by mighty sobs, entirely buried her face and bosom in my couch. Meantime, moved at once by pity and apprehension, I bade her keep a good heart, and be quite easy on either head. For, I assured her, not one of us would divulge the mysteries, and moreover, if the god had revealed any extraordinary means of curing her ague, we would second divine providence, even if it involved danger to ourselves.

The woman cheered up at this promise, and fell to kissing me thick and fast, and changing from tears to laughter, combed back with her fingers some stray locks that had escaped from behind my ears. "I make truce with you," she said, "and withdraw my case against you. But if you had not agreed about the remedy I am seeking, I had a posse of men all ready for to-morrow to avenge my wrongs and vindicate my honour.

"Contempt is hateful; what I love is power,
  To work my will at my own place and hour;
  A wise man's scorn bends the most stubborn will,
  The noblest victor he who spares to kill."

Next, clapping her hands together, she suddenly burst into such a fit of laughter as quite alarmed us. The maid who had entered first followed suit, and was followed in turn by the little girl who had come in along with Quartilla.

The whole place re-echoed with their forced merriment; meantime, seeing no reason for this rapid change of mood, we stand staring now at each other, now at the women. At length says Quartilla, "I have given express orders that no mortal be admitted into this inn to-day, that you may, without interruption, apply the remedy for my ague."

"At this declaration Ascyltos stood for a time appalled; for myself, I turned colder than a Gallic winter, and was unable to utter a word. Still our numbers somewhat reassured me against any disaster. After all, they were only three weak women, quite incapable of any serious assault on us, who if we had nothing else manly about us, were at least of the male sex. Anyway we were all ready prepared for the fray; in fact I had already so arranged the couples, that if it came to a fight, I should myself tackle Quartilla, Ascyltos the waiting-maid, Giton the girl.

In the middle of these reflections, up came Quartilla to me to be cured of her ague; but finding herself sadly disappointed, she flung out of the house in a rage. Returning after a little, she had us seized by some unknown bravos and carried off to a magnificent palace.

CHAPTER FOUR

At this crisis amazement and consternation quite broke our spirit, certain death seeming to stare us miserably in the face. "I beseech you, lady," I cried, "if you have any sinister design, put us out of our misery at once; we have done nothing so heinous as to deserve torturing to death." The maid, whose name was Psyche, now carefully spread a rug on the marble floor, and endeavoured to rouse my member into activity, but it lay cold as a thousand deaths could make it. Ascyltos had muffled his head in his mantle, having doubtless learned from experience the peril of meddling with other people's secrets. Meantime Psyche produced two ribbons from her bosom, and proceeded to tie our hands with one and our feet with the other; finding myself thus fettered, "This is not the way," I protested, "for your mistress to get what she wants." "Granted," replied the maid; "but I have other remedies to my hand, and surer ones." So saying, she brought me a goblet full of satyrion, and with quips and cranks and a host of wonderful tales of its virtues, induced me to drain off nearly the whole of the liquor. Then, because he had slighted her overtures a little before, she poured what was left of the stuff over Ascyltos's back without his noticing. The latter, seeing the stream of her eloquence dried up, exclaimed, "Well! and am I not thought worthy to have a drink too?" Betrayed by my laughter, the girl clapped her hands and cried, "Why! I've given it you already, young man; you've had the whole draught all to yourself." "What!" put in Quartilla, "has Encolpius drunk up all our stock of satyrion?" and her sides shook with pretty merriment. Eventually not even Giton could contain his mirth, particularly when the little girl threw her arms round his neck, and gave the boy, who showed no signs of reluctance, a thousand kisses.

We should have cried out for help in our unhappy plight, but there was no one to hear us, and besides Psyche pricked my cheeks with her hair pin every time I tried to call upon my fellow countrymen for succour, while at the same time the other girl threatened Ascyltos with a brush dipped in satyrion. Finally there entered a catamite, tricked out in a coat of chestnut frieze, and wearing a sash, who would alternately writhe his buttocks and bump against us, and beslaver us with most evil-smelling kisses, until Quartilla, holding a whalebone wand in her hand and with skirts tucked up, ordered him to give the poor fellows quarter. Then we all three swore the most solemn oaths the horrid secret should die with us.

Next a company of wrestlers appeared, who rubbed us over with the proper gymnastic oil, which was very refreshing. This removed our fatigue, (we resumed the dinner clothes that we had taken off) and we were then conducted into the adjoining room, where the couches were laid and all preparations made for an elegant feast in the most sumptuous style. We were requested to take our places, and the banquet opened with some wonderful hors d'oeuvres, while the Falernian flowed like water. A number of other courses followed, and we were all but falling asleep, when Quartilla cried, "Come, come! can you think of sleep, when you know this livelong night is owed to the service of Priapus?"

Ascyltos was so worn out with all he had gone through he could not keep his eyes open a moment longer, and the waiting-maid, whom he had scorned and slighted, now proceeded to daub his face all over with streaks of soot, and bepaint his lips and shoulders, as he lay unconscious.

I too, tired with the persecutions I had endured, was just enjoying forty winks, as they say, while all the household, within doors and without, had copied my example. Some lay sprawling about the diners' feet, others propped against the walls, while others snored head to head right on the threshold. The oil in the lamps had burned low, and they shed a feeble, dying light, when two Syrian slaves came into the banquet-room to crib a flagon of wine. As they were greedily fighting for it and scuffling amongst the silver, it parted and broke in two. At the same moment the table with the silver plate collapsed, and a goblet falling from perhaps a greater height than the rest, struck the waiting-maid who was lying exhausted on a couch underneath and cut her head open. She screamed out at the blow, at once discovering the thieves and awakening some of the drunkards. The Syrians, thus caught in the act, threw themselves with one accord onto a couch, and started snoring as if they had been asleep ever so long.

By this time the chief butler had wakened up and put fresh oil into the expiring lamps, while the other slaves after rubbing their eyes a bit, had resumed their posts, and presently a symbal-player came in and roused us all up with a clash of her instruments. So the banquet was resumed, and Quartilla challenged us to start a fresh carouse, the tinkle of the cymbals still further stimulating her reckless gaiety.

The next to appear is a catamite, the silliest of mankind and quite worthy of the house, who beat his hands together, gave a groan, and then spouted the following delightful effusion:

> "Who hath a pathic lust,
>   With Delian vice accurst;
> Who loves the pliant thigh,
>   Quick hand and wanton sigh;
> Come hither, come hither, come hither,
>   Here shall he see
>   Gross beasts as he,
>   Lechers of every feather!"

Then, his poetry exhausted, he spat a most stinking kiss in my face; before long he mounted on the couch where I lay and exposed me by force in spite of my resistance. He laboured hard and long to bring up my member, but in vain. Streams of gummy paint and sweat poured from his heated brow, and such a lot of chalk filled the wrinkles of his cheeks, you might

have thought his face was an old dilapidated wall with
the plaster crumbling away in the rain.

I could no longer restrain my tears, but driven to
the last extremity of disgust, "I ask you, lady," I cried,
"is this the 'night-cap' (ambasicoetas) you promised
me?" At this she clapped her hands daintily, exclaiming. "Oh you clever boy! what a pretty wit you have!
Of course you didn't know 'night-cap' is another name
for a catamite?" Then, that my comrade might not
miss his share too, I asked her, "Now, on your con-
science, is Ascyltos to be the only guest in the room
to keep holiday!" "So?" she cried, "why! let Ascyltos have his 'nightcap' too!" In obedience to her
order, the catamite now changed his mount, and trans-
ferring his attentions to my friend, set to grinding him
under his buttocks and smothering him with lecherous
kisses.

All this while Giton had been standing by, laughing
as if his sides would split. Now Quartilla, catching
sight of him, asked with eager curiosity, whose lad he
was. When I told her he was my little favourite, "Why
hasn't he kissed me then?" she cried, and calling him
to her glued her lips to his. Next minute she slipped
her hand under his clothes, and pulling out his un-
practised tool, she observed, "This will be a very
pretty whet to-morrow to our naughty appetite. For
to-day,—'After such a dainty dish, I will taste no common fish!'"

Just as she was saying this, Psyche approached her
mistress laughingly and whispered something in her
ear. "Yes! yes!" exclaimed Quartilla, "a capital idea!

why should not our little Pannychis lose her maiden-head! 'tis an excellent opportunity." Immediately they brought in a pretty enough little girl, and who did not appear to be more than seven years old, the same child who had accompanied Quartilla on her first visit to our room at the inn. So amid general applause and indeed at the special request of the company, they be-gan the bridal preparations. I was horrified, and de-clared that, while on the one hand Giton, who was a very modest boy, was quite unequal to such naughti-ness, on the other Pannychis was far too young to en-dure the treatment a woman must expect. "Why!" said Quartilla, "is the girl any younger than I was when I first submitted to a man? May Juno, my patroness, desert me, if I can mind the time when I was a maid. As a child I was naughty with little boys of my own age, and presently as the years rolled by, with bigger lads, till I reached my present time of life. Hence I suppose the proverb that says: 'Who carried the calf, may well carry the bull.'"

Fearing my favourite might get into greater troubles if I were not there, I got up too to assist at the wed-ding ceremony.

By this time Psyche had thrown the bridal veil over the child's head; our pathic friend was marching in front with a torch; a long procession of drunken women followed, clapping their hands, having pre-viously decked the marriage bed with a splendid cover-let. Then Quartilla, fired by the wanton pleasantry, likewise rose from the table, and seizing Giton drew him into the chamber. The lad was not at all loath to go, and even the child manifested very little fear or reluctance at the name of matrimony. In due course when they were in bed and the door shut, we sat down on the threshold of the nuptial chamber, and first of all Quartilla applied an inquisitive eye to a crack in the door contrived for some such naughty purpose, and watched their childish dalliance with lecherous intentness. She drew me gently to her side to enjoy the same spectacle, and our faces being close together as we looked, she would, at every interval in the performance, twist her lips sideways to meet mine, continually pecking at me with a sort of furtive kisses.

Suddenly in the midst of these proceedings a prodigious thumping made itself heard at the entrance door, and whilst everybody was wondering what the unexpected interruption might mean, we saw a soldier come in, one of the nightwatch, with a drawn sword in his hand and surrounded by a crowd of young men. The fellow glared about him with bloodshot eyes and braggadocio airs; presently spying Quartilla, he cried, "What have we here, abandoned woman? How dare you make game of me with your falsehoods and cheat me out of the night you promised me? But you shan't go unpunished, I can tell you; you and your lover shall find out you have a man to deal with." Obeying the soldier's orders, his comrades now bind Quartilla and myself together, mouth to mouth, bosom to bosom, and thigh to thigh, in the midst of shouts of laughter. Then the catamite, still by the soldier's order, began to beslaver me horribly all over with the odious kisses of his stinking lips—a treatment I had no means either of escaping from or avoiding. Before long he debauched me, and worked his full will upon my body. Meantime, the satyrion I had drunk a while before, stirring every fibre to lasciviousness, I began to perform vigorously on Quartilla, while she fired with a like wantonness, showed no repugnance to the game. The young soldiers burst into fits of laughter at the ludicrous performance; for, while myself mounted by a vile catamite, involuntarily and almost without knowing what I was at, I kept moving to him just as fast and furiously as Quartilla was wriggling under me.

At this moment Pannychis, unaccustomed at her tender age to love's ardours, raised a sudden cry of pain and consternation, which the soldier heard. The poor child was in the act of being ravished, and the triumphant Giton had won a not bloodless victory. Roused by the sight, the man rushed at them, and clipped now Pannychis, now Giton, and now both of them together, in his sturdy arms. The girl burst into tears and besought him to take pity on her tender years; but her prayers were entirely unavailing, the soldier being only the more excited by her childish charms. All Pannychis could do was to throw a veil over her face and resign herself to endure whatever fate might bring her.

But at this crisis who should come to the unfortunate child's rescue, as if she had dropped from the sky, but the very same old woman who had beguiled me the day I was inquiring my road home? She burst into the house with loud cries, declaring that a band of robbers was prowling about the neighbourhood, while peaceable citizens were crying in vain for help, the guard being asleep or busy with their victuals,—at any rate nowhere to be found. The soldier, much disturbed at what she said, fled precipitately from the house and his companions following his example, freed Pannychis from the impending danger and relieved us all of our terror.

So weary was I by this time of Quartilla's lecherousness that I began to revolve means of escape. I opened my mind to Ascyltos, who was only too pleased to hear of my purpose, longing to be rid of Psyche's importunities. The thing would have been plain sailing enough, had not Giton been locked up in the chamber; for we wished to take him with us and save him from the viciousness of these strumpets. We were anxiously debating the point when Pannychis fell out of bed, and her weight dragged Giton after her. He was unhurt, but the child having given her head a slight knock, raised such an outcry that Quartilla in a fright rushed headlong into the room, and so gave us an opportunity to escape. Without an instant's delay, we fly with all speed to our inn and throwing ourselves into bed, spent the rest of the night in security.

Going abroad next day, we came upon two of Quartilla's fellows who had kidnapped us to her palace. No sooner did Ascyltos clap eyes on the rascals than he vigorously attacked one of them, and after beating and seriously wounding him, came to my help against the other. But this last bore himself so stoutly that he managed to wound us both, though only slightly, escaping himself without a scratch.

CHAPTER FIVE

THE third day had now arrived, the date appointed for the free banquet at Trimalchio's; but with so many wounds as we had, we deemed it better policy to fly than to remain where we were. So we made the best of our way to our inn, and our hurts being only skin-deep after all, we lay in bed and dressed them with wine and oil.

Still one of the rascals was lying on the ground disabled, and we were afraid we might yet be discovered. Whilst we were still debating sadly with ourselves how we might best escape the storm, a slave of Agamemnon's broke into our trembling conclave, crying, "What! don't you recollect whose entertainment it is this day?—Trimalchio's, a most elegant personage; he has a time-piece in his dining-room and a trumpeter specially provided for the purpose keeps him constantly informed how much of his lifetime is gone." So, forgetting all our troubles, we proceed to make a careful toilette, and bid Giton, who had always hitherto been very ready to act as servant, to attend us at the bath.

Meantime in our gala dresses, we began to stroll about, or rather to amuse ourselves by approaching the different groups of ballplayers. Amongst these we all of a sudden catch sight of a baldheaded old

man in a russet tunic, playing ball amid a troupe of
long-haired boys. It was not however so much the
boys, though these were well worth looking at, that
drew us to the spot, as the master himself, who wore
sandals and was playing with green balls. He never
stooped for a ball that had once touched ground, but
an attendant stood by with a sackful, and supplied the
players as they required them. We noticed other
novelties too. For two eunuchs were stationed at opposite points of the circle, one holding a silver chamber-
pot, while the other counted the balls,—not those that
were in play and flying from hand to hand, but such as
fell on the floor.

We were still admiring these refinements of elegance when Menelaus runs up, saying, "See! that's the
gentleman you are to dine with; why! this is really
nothing else than a prelude to the entertainment." He
had not finished speaking when Trimalchio snapped his
fingers, and at the signal the eunuch held out the
chamber-pot for him, without his ever stopping play.
After easing his bladder, he called for water, and
having dipped his hands momentarily in the bowl,
dried them on one of the lads' hair.

There was no time to notice every detail; so we
entered the bath, and after stewing in the sweating-
room, passed instantly into the cold chamber. Trimalchio, after being drenched with unguent, was being
rubbed down, not however with ordinary towels but
with pieces of blanketing of the softest and finest
wool. Meanwhile three bagnio doctors were swilling
Falernian under his eyes; and seeing how the fellows

were brawling over their liquor and spilling most of it, Trimalchio declared it was a libation they were making in his particular honour.

Presently muffled in a wraprascal of scarlet frieze, he was placed in a litter, preceded by four running-footmen in tinselled liveries, and a wheeled chair, in which his favourite rode, a little old young man, sore-eyed and uglier even than his master. As the latter was borne along, a musician took up his place at his head with a pair of miniature flutes, and played softly to him, as if he were whispering secrets in his ear. Full of wonder we follow the procession and arrive at the same moment as Agamemnon at the outer door, on one of the pillars of which was suspended a tablet bearing the words:

ANY SLAVE
GOING ABROAD WITHOUT THE MASTER'S
PERMISSION
SHALL RECEIVE ONE HUNDRED LASHES

Just within the vestibule stood the doorkeeper, dressed in green with a cherry-coloured sash, busy picking pease in a silver dish. Over the threshold hung a gold cage with a black and white magpie in it, which greeted visitors on their entrance.

But as I was staring open-eyed at all these fine sights, I came near tumbling backwards and breaking my legs. For to the left hand as you entered, and not far from the porter's lodge, a huge chained dog was depicted on the wall, and written above in capital letters: 'WARE DOG! 'WARE DOG! My com-

panions made merry at my expense; but soon regain-
ing confidence, I fell to examining the other paintings
on the walls. One of these represented a slave-market,
the men standing up with labels round their necks,
while in another Trimalchio himself, wearing long
hair, holding a caduceus in his hand and led by
Minerva, was entering Rome. Further on, the ingenious painter had shown him learning accounts, and
presently made steward of the estate, each incident being made clear by explanatory inscriptions. Lastly at
the extreme end of the portico, Mercury was lifting
the hero by the chin and placing him on the highest
seat of a tribunal. Fortune stood by with her cornu-
copia, and the three Fates, spinning his destiny with
a golden thread.

I noticed likewise in the portico a gang of running-
footmen exercising under a trainer. Moreover I saw
in a corner a vast awmry; and in a shrine inside were
ranged Lares of silver, and a marble statue of Venus,
and a golden casket of ample dimensions, in which
they said the great man's first beard was preserved.
I now asked the hall-keeper what were the subjects
of the frescoes in the atrium itself. "The Iliad and
Odyssey," he replied, "and on your left the combat
of gladiators given under Laenas."

We had no opportunity of examining the numerous
paintings more minutely, having by this time reached
the banquet-hall, at the outer door of which the house-
steward sat receiving accounts. But the thing that
surprised me most was to notice on the doorposts of
the apartment fasces and axes fixed up, the lower part

terminating in an ornament resembling the bronze beak of a ship, on which was inscribed:

> To Gaius Pompeius Trimalchio,
> Augustal Sevir
> Cinnamus His Treasurer.

Underneath this inscription hung a lamp with two lights, depending from the vaulting. Two other tablets were attached to the doorposts. One, if my memory serves me, bore the following inscription:

> On December Thirtieth and
> Thirty-First
> Our Master Gaius Dines Abroad.

The other showed the phases of the moon and the seven planets, while lucky and unlucky days were marked by distinctive studs.

When, sated with all these fine sights, we were just making for the entrance of the banquet-hall, one of the slaves, stationed there for the purpose, called out, "Right foot first!" Not unnaturally there was a moment's hesitation, for fear one of us should break the rule. But this was not all; for just as we stepped out in line right leg foremost, another slave, stripped of his outer garments, threw himself before our feet, beseeching us to save him from punishment. Not indeed that his fault was a very serious one; in point of fact the Intendant's clothes had been stolen when in his charge at the bath,—a matter of ten sesterces or so at the outside. So facing about, still right foot in front, we approached the Intendant, who was counting gold in the hall, and asked him to forgive the poor man. He looked up haughtily and said, "It's not so much the loss that annoys me as the rascal's carelessness. He has lost my dinner robes, which a client gave me on my birthday,—genuine Tyrian purple, I assure you, though only once dipped. But there! I will pardon the delinquent at your request."

Deeply grateful for so signal a favour, we now returned to the banquet-hall, where we were met by the same slave for whom we had interceded, who to our astonishment overwhelmed us with a perfect storm of kisses, thanking us again and again for our humanity. "Indeed," he cried, "you shall presently know who it is you have obliged; the master's wine is the cup-bearer's thank-offering."

Well! at last we take our places, Alexandrian slave-boys pouring snow water over our hands, and others succeeding them to wash our feet and cleanse our toe nails with extreme dexterity. Not even while engaged in this unpleasant office were they silent, but sang away over their work. I had a mind to try whether all the house servants were singers, and accordingly asked for a drink of wine. Instantly an attendant was at my side, pouring out the liquor to the accompaniment of the same sort of shrill recitative. Demand what you would, it was the same; you might have supposed yourself among a troupe of pantomime actors rather than at a respectable citizen's table.

Then the preliminary course was served in very elegant style. For all were now at table except Trimalchio, for whom the first place was reserved,—by a re-

versal of ordinary usage. Among the other hors
d'oeuvres stood a little ass of Corinthian bronze with
a packsaddle holding olives, white olives on one side,
black on the other. The animal was flanked right
and left by silver dishes, on the rim of which Trimalchio's name was engraved and the weight. On arches
built up in the form of miniature bridges were dormice
seasoned with honey and poppy-seed. There were
sausages too smoking hot on a silver grill, and underneath (to imitate coals) Syrian plums and pomegranate seeds.

We were in the middle of these elegant trifles when
Trimalchio himself was carried in to the sound of
music, and was bolstered up among a host of tiny
cushions,—a sight that set one or two indiscreet guests
laughing. And no wonder; his bald head poked up
out of a scarlet mantle, his neck was closely muffled,
and over all was laid a napkin with a broad purple
stripe or laticlave, and long fringes hanging down either
side. Moreover he wore on the little finger of his
left hand a massive ring of silver gilt, and on the last
joint of the next finger a smaller ring, apparently of
solid gold, but starred superficially with little ornaments of steel. Nay! to show this was not the whole
of his magnificence, his left arm was bare, and displayed a gold bracelet and an ivory circlet with a
sparkling clasp to put it on.

After picking his teeth with a silver toothpick, "My
friends," he began, "I was far from desirous of coming to table just yet, but that I might not keep you
waiting by my absence, I have sadly interfered with

my own amusement. But will you permit me to finish
my game?" A slave followed him in, carrying a
draught-board of terebinth wood and crystal dice. One
special bit of refinement I noticed; instead of the ordinary black and white men he had medals of gold and
silver respectively.

Meantime, whilst he is exhausting the vocabulary
of a tinker over the game, and we are still at the hors
d'oeuvres, a dish was brought in with a basket on it,
in which lay a wooden hen, her wings outspread round
her as if she were sitting. Instantly a couple of slaves
came up, and to the sound of lively music began to
search the straw, and pulling out a lot of pea-fowl's
eggs one after the other, handed them round to the
company. Trimalchio turns his head at this, saying,
"My friends, it was by my orders the hen was set on
the peafowl's eggs yonder; but by God! I am very
much afraid they are half-hatched. Still we can but
try whether they are still eatable." For our part, we
take our spoons, which weighed at least half a pound
each, and break the eggs, which were made of paste.
I was on the point of throwing mine away, for I thought
I discerned a chick inside. But when I overheard a
veteran guest saying, "There should be something
good here!" I further investigated the shell, and
found a very fine fat beccafico swimming in yolk of egg
flavoured with pepper.

Trimalchio had by this time stopped his game and
been helped to all the dishes before us. He had just
announced in a loud voice that any of us who wanted
a second supply of honeyed wine had only to ask for

it, when suddenly at a signal from the band, the hors d'oeuvres are whisked away by a troupe of slaves, all singing too. But in the confusion a silver dish happened to fall and a slave picked it up again from the floor; this Trimalchio noticed, and boxing the fellow's ears, rated him soundly and ordered him to throw it down again. Then a groom came in and began to sweep up the silver along with the other refuse with his besom.

He was succeeded by two long-haired Ethiopians, carrying small leather skins, like the fellows that water the sand in the amphitheatre, who poured wine over our hands; for no one thought of offering water.

After being duly complimented on this refinement, our host cried out, "Fair play's a jewel!" and accordingly ordered a separate table to be assigned to each guest. "In this way," he said, "by preventing any crowding, the stinking servants won't make us so hot."

Simultaneously there were brought in a number of wine-jars of glass carefully stoppered with plaster, and having labels attached to their necks reading:

FALERNIAN; OPIMIAN VINTAGE
ONE HUNDRED YEARS OLD.

Whilst we were reading the labels, Trimalchio ejaculated, striking his palms together, "Alackaday! to think wine is longer lived than poor humanity! Well! bumpers then! There's life in wine. 'Tis the right Opimian, I give you my word. I didn't bring out any so good yesterday, and much better men than you were dining with me."

So we drank our wine and admired all this luxury in good set terms. Then the slave brought in a silver skeleton, so artfully fitted with its articulations and vertebræ were all movable and would turn and twist in any direction. After he had tossed this once or twice on the table, causing the loosely jointed limbs to take various postures, Trimalchio moralized thus:

Alas! how less than naught are we;
Fragile life's thread, and brief our day!
What this is now, we all shall be;
Drink and make merry while you may.

CHAPTER SIX

OUR applause was interrupted by the second course, which did not by any means come up to our expectations. Still the oddity of the thing drew the eyes of all. An immense circular tray bore the twelve signs of the zodiac displayed round the circumference, on each of which the Manoiple or Arranger had placed a dish of suitable and appropriate viands: on the Ram ram's-head pease, on the Bull a piece of beef, on the Twins fried testicles and kidneys, on the Crab simply a Crown, on the Lion African figs, on a Virgin a sow's haslet, (on Libra a balance with a tart in one scale and a cheese-cake in the other, on Scorpio a small sea-fish, on Sagittarius an eye-seeker, on Capricornus a lobster, on Aquarius a wild goose, on Pisces two mullets. In the middle was a sod of green turf) cut to shape and supporting a honeycomb. Meanwhile an Egyptian slave was carrying bread round in a miniature oven of silver, crooning to himself in a horrible voice a song in praise of wine and laserpitium.

Seeing us look rather blank at the idea of attacking such common fare, Trimalchio cried, "I pray you gentlemen, begin; the best of your dinner is before you." No sooner had he spoken than four fellows ran prancing in, keeping time to the music, and whipped off the top part of the tray. This done, we

beheld underneath, on a second tray in fact, stuffed
capons, a sow's paps, and as a centrepiece a hare fitted
with wings to represent Pegasus. We noticed besides
four figures of Marsyas, one at each corner of the tray,
carrying little wine-skins which spouted out peppered
fish-sauce over the fishes swimming in the Channel
of the dish.

We all join in the applause started by the domestics
and laughingly fall to on the choice viands. Trimalchio, as pleased as anybody with a device of the sort,
now called out, "Cut!" Instantly the Carver advanced, and posturing in time to the music, sliced up
the joint with such antics you might have thought him
a jockey struggling to pull off a chariot-race to the
thunder of the organ. Yet all the while Trimalchio
kept repeating in a wheedling voice, "Cut! Cut!"
For my part, suspecting there was some pretty jest
connected with this everlasting reiteration of the word,
I made no bones about asking the question of the guest
who sat immediately above me. He had often wit-
nessed similar scenes and told me at once, "You see
the man who is carving; well; his name is Cut. The
master is calling and commanding him at one and the
same time."

Unable to eat any more, I now turned towards my
neighbour in order to glean what information I could,
and after indulging in a string of general remarks,
presently asked him, "Who is that lady bustling up and
down the room yonder?" "Trimalchio's lady," he replied; "her name is Fortunata, and she counts her coin
by the bushelful! Before? what was she before?

Why! my dear Sir! saving your respect, you would
have been mighty sorry to take bread from her hand.
Now, by hook or by crook, she's got to heaven, and
is Trimalchio's factotum. In fact if she told him it was
dark night at high noon, he'd believe her. The man's
rolling in riches, and really can't tell what he has and
what he hasn't got; still his good lady looks keenly
after everything, and is on the spot where you least
expect to see her. She's temperate, sober and well
advised, but she has a sharp tongue of her own and
chatters like a magpie between the bed-curtains. When
she likes a man, she likes him; and when she doesn't,
well! she doesn't.

"As for Trimalchio, his lands reach as far as the
kites fly, and his money breeds money. I tell you, he
has more coin lying idle in his porter's lodge than
would make another man's whole fortune. Slaves!
why, heaven and earth! I don't believe one in ten
knows his own master by sight. For all that, there's
never a one of the fine fellows a word of his wouldn't
send scutting into the nearest rat-hole. And don't you
imagine he ever buys anything; every mortal thing is
home grown,—wool, rosin, pepper; call for hen's milk
and he'd supply you! As a matter of fact his wool was
not first rate originally; but he purchased rams at
Tarentum and so improved the breed. To get home-
made Attic honey he had bees imported direct from
Athens, hoping at the same time to benefit the native
insects a bit by a cross with the Greek fellows. Why!
only the other day he wrote to India for mushroom
spawn. He has not a single mule but was got by a

wild ass. You see all these mattresses; never a one that is not stuffed with the finest wool, purple or scarlet as the case may be. Lucky, lucky dog!

"And look you, don't you turn up your nose at the other freedmen, his fellows. They're very warm men. You see the one lying last on the last couch yonder? He's worth his eight hundred thousand any of these days. A self-made man; once upon a time he carried wood on his own two shoulders. They do say,—I don't know how true it may be, but I've been told so,—he snatched an Incubo's hat, and so discovered a treasure. I grudge no man's good fortune, whatever God has seen good to give him. He'll still take a box o' the ear for all that, and keeps a keen eye on the main chance. Only the other day he placarded his house with this bill:

C. POMPEIUS DIOGENES
IS PREPARED TO LET HIS GARRET
FROM JULY FIRST,
HAVING BOUGHT THE HOUSE HIMSELF.

"But the other man yonder, occupying a freedman's place, what of him? Was he originally very well to do?" "I have not a word to say against him. He was master once of a cool million, but he came to sad grief. I don't suppose he has a hair on his head unmortgaged. Not that it was any fault of his; there never was a better man, but his rascally freedmen swindled him out of everything. Let me tell you, when the hospitable pot stops boiling, and fortune has once taken the turn, friends soon make themselves scarce." "What was the honourable calling he followed, that you see him brought to this?" "He was an undertaker. He used to dine like a King,—boars in pastry, cakes of every sort and game galore, cooks and pastry-cooks without end. More wine was spilt under his table than another man has in his cellar. A dream—not a life for a mere mortal man! Even when his affairs were getting shaky, for fear his creditors might think he was in difficulties, he posted this noticed of sale:

C. JULIUS PROCULUS
WILL PUT UP TO AUCTION
AN ASSORTMENT
OF HIS SUPERFLUOUS FURNITURE."

This agreeable gossip was here interrupted by Trimalchio; for the second course had now been removed, and the company being merry with wine began to engage in general conversation. Our host then, lying back on his elbow and addressing the company, said, "I hope you will all do justice to this wine; you must make the fish swim again. Come, come, do you suppose I was going to rest content with the dinner you saw boxed up under the cover of the tray just now? 'Is Ulysses no better known?' Well, well! even at table we mustn't forget our scholarship. Peace to my worthy patron's bones, who was pleased to make me a man amongst men. For truly there is nothing can be set before me that will nonplus me by its novelty. For instance the meaning of that tray just now can be easily enough explained. This heaven in which dwell the twelve gods resolves itself into twelve different configurations, and presently becomes the Ram. So whosoever is born under this sign has many flocks and herds and much wool, a hard head into the bargain, a shameless brow and a sharp horn. Most of your schoolmen and pettifoggers are born under this sign."

We recommended the learned expounder's graceful erudition, and he went on to add: "Next the whole sky becomes Bull; then are born obstinate fellows and neatherds and such as think of nothing but filling their own bellies. Under the Twins are born horses in a pair, oxen in a yoke, men blessed with a sturdy brace of testicles, all who manage to keep in with both sides. I was born under the Crab myself. Wherefore I stand on many feet, and have many possessions both by sea and land; for the Crab is equally adapted to either element. And this is why I never put anything on that sign, so as not to eclipse my horoscope. Under the Lion are born great eaters and wasters, and all who love to domineer; under the Virgin, women and run-aways and jailbirds; under the Scales, butchers and perfumers and all retail traders; under the Scorpion, poisoners and cut-throats; under the Archer, squint-eyed folks, who look at the greens and whip off with the bacon; under Capricorn, the 'horny-handed sons of toil'; under Aquarius or the Waterman, innkeepers and pumpkin-heads; under Pisces, or the Fishes, fine cooks and fine talkers. Thus the world goes round like a mill, and is for ever at some mischief, whether making men or marring them. But about the sod of turf you see in the middle, and the honeycomb atop of it, I have a good reason to show too. Our mother Earth is in the middle, round-about like an egg, and has all good things in her inside, like a honeycomb!"

"Clever! clever!" we cry in chorus, and with hands uplifted to the ceiling, swear Hipparchus and Aratus were not to be named in the same breath with him. This lasted till fresh servants entered and spread carpets before the couches, embroidered with pictures of fowling nets, prickers with their hunting spears, and sporting gear of all kinds. We were still at a loss what to expect when a tremendous shout was raised outside the doors, and lo! and behold, a pack of Laconian dogs came careering round and round the very table. These were succeeded by another huge tray, on which lay a wild boar of the largest size, with a cap on its head, while from the tushes hung two little baskets of woven palm leaves, one full of Syrian dates, the other of Theban. Round it were little piglets of baked sweetmeats, as if at suck, to show it was a sow we had before us; and these were gifts to be taken home with them by the guests.

To carve the dish however, it was not this time our friend Cut who appeared, the same who had dismembered the capons, but a great bearded fellow, wearing leggings and a shaggy jerkin. Drawing his hunting knife, he made a furious lunge and gashed open the boar's flank, from which there flew out a number of field-fares. Fowlers stood ready with their rods and immediately caught the birds as they fluttered about the table. Then Trimalchio directed each guest to be given his bird, and this done, added "Look what elegant acorns this wild-wood pig fed on." Instantly slaves ran to the baskets that were suspended from the animal's tushes and divided the two kind of dates in equal proportions among the diners.

Meantime, sitting as I did a little apart, I was led into a thousand conjectures to account for the boar's being brought in with a cap on. So after exhausting all sorts of absurd guesses, I resolved to ask my former "philosopher and friend" to explain the difficulty that tormented me so. "Why!" said he, "your own servant could tell you that much. Riddle? it's as plain as daylight. The boar was presented with his freedom at yesterday's dinner; he appeared at the end of the meal and the company gave him his conge. Therefore today he comes back to table as a freedman." I cursed my own stupidity, and asked no more questions, for fear of their thinking I had never dined with good company before.

We were still conversing, when a pretty boy entered, his head wreathed with vine-leaves and ivy, announcing himself now as Bromius, anon as Lyaeus and Evous. He proceeded to hand round grapes in a small basket, and recited in the shrillest of voices some verses of his master's composition. Trimalchio turned round at the sound, and, "Dionysus," said he, "be free (Liber)!" The lad snatched the cap from the boar's head and stuck it on his own. Then Trimalchio went on again, "Well! you'll not deny," he cried, "I have a Father Liber (a freeborn father) of my own." We praised Trimalchio's joke, and heartily kissed the fortunate lad, as he went round the company to receive our congratulations.

CHAPTER SEVEN

At the end of this course Trimalchio left the table to relieve himself, and so finding ourselves free from the constraint of his overbearing presence, we began to indulge in a little friendly conversation. Accordingly Dama began first, after calling for a cup of wine. "A day! what is a day?" he exclaimed, "before you can turn round, it's night again! So really you can't do better than go straight from bed to board. Fine cold weather we've been having; why! even my bath has hardly warmed me. But truly hot liquor is a good clothier. I've been drinking bumpers, and I'm down-right fuddled. The wine has got into my head."

Seleucus then struck into the talk: "I don't bathe every day," he said; "your systematic bather's a mere fuller. Water's got teeth, and melts the heart away, a little every day; but there! when I've fortified my belly with a cup of mulled wine, I say 'Go hang!' to the cold. Indeed I couldn't bathe to-day, for I've been to a funeral. A fine fellow he was too, good old Chrysanthus, but he's given up the ghost now. He was calling me just this moment, only just this moment; I could fancy myself talking to him now. Alas! alas! what are we but blown bladders on two legs? We're not worth as much as flies! they are some use, but we're no better than bubbles." "He wasn't careful enough in his diet?" "I tell you, for five whole days not one drop of water, or one crumb of bread, passed his lips. Nevertheless he has joined the majority. The doctors killed him,—or rather his day was come; the very best of doctors is only a satisfaction to the mind. Anyhow he was handsomely buried, on his own best bed, with good blankets. The wailing was first class, —he did a trifle of manumission before he died; though no doubt his wife's tears were a bit forced. A pity he always treated her so well. But woman! woman's of the kite kind. No man ought ever to do 'em a good turn; just as well pitch it in the well at once. Old love's an eating sore!"

He was getting tiresome, and Phileros broke in: "Let's talk of the living. He's got his deserts, whatever they were; he lived well and died well, what has he to complain about? He started with next to nothing, and was ready to the last to pick a farthing out of a dunghill with his teeth. So he grew and grew, like a honeycomb. Upon my word I believe he left a round hundred million behind him, and all in ready money. But I'll tell you the actual facts, for I'm the soul of truth, as they say. He had a rough tongue, and a ready one, and was quarrelsomeness personified. Now his brother was a fine fellow and a true friend, with a free hand and keeping a liberal table. Just at the beginning he had a bad bird to pluck, but the very first vintage set him on his legs, for he sold his wine at his own price. But the thing that chiefly made him lift up his head in the world was getting an inheritance, out of which he managed to prig a

good deal more than was really left him. And that log
Chrysanthus, falling out with his brother, has positively left all his property to I don't know what scum
of the earth. He goes too far, say I, who goes outside his own kith and kin. But he had a lot of over-
wise interfering servants, who proved his ruin. A man
will never do well, who believes all he's told too readily,
especially a man in business. Yet it's fair to say he
did well enough all his life, getting what was never
meant for him. Evidently one of Fortune's favourites,
in whose hands lead turns to gold. But that's simple
enough, when everything runs on wheels exactly as you
want it to. How old, think you, was he when he
died? Seventy and over. But he was as tough as
horn; he carried his age well, and he was still as black
as a crow. I knew him when he was a pretty loose fish,
and he was lecherous to the last. Upon my soul I
don't believe he left a living thing in his house alone,
down to the dog. A great lover of lads, indeed a man
of universal talents and tastes. Not that I blame him;
this was all the gain he carried out of the world with
him."

So much for Phileros; then Ganymede began: "Yes!
you talk away," he said, "about things that concern
neither heaven nor earth, but no one ever thinks of
the pinch of famine that's upon us. I swear I couldn't
come across a mouthful of bread this day. And how
the drought holds! Starvation's been the word for
a whole twelvemonth now. Bad cess to the Ædiles,
who are in collusion with the bakers—'you scratch my
back, and I'll scratch yours.' And so poor folks suffer;

for you rich fellows' jawbones keep feast-day all the
year round. Ah! if only we had those lion-hearted
chaps I found here, when first I came from Asia. That
was something like living. 'Twas like the midlands of
Sicily for plenty, and they used to batter those vam-
pires about so that Jupiter positively hated them.
Why! I can remember Safinius; he used to live at the
Old Arch when I was a boy. It was a peppercorn, I
tell you, not a man. Wherever he went, he made the
ground smoke under him. An upright, downright
honest man, and a trusty friend, one you might con-
fidently play mora with in the dark. But in Court,
how he pounded 'em down, one and all; he didn't talk
in figures of speech, not he, but straight out. Then
when he pleaded in the Forum, his voice would swell
out like a trumpet, though he never sweated nor spat.
I believe myself he had a smack of Asiatic blood in
him. And how civil he was to return our bows and
give each man his name, just as if he'd been one of
ourselves. So in those days provisions were dirt cheap.
A halfpenny loaf,—when you'd bought it, you couldn't
have finished it, with another man to help you! Now,
—I've seen a bullock's eye bigger. Alas! alas! things
get worse and worse every day, and this city of ours
is growing like a cow's tail, backwards. Why ever
have we an Ædile not worth three figs, who thinks
more of a halfpenny than of all our lives. So he sits
at home and rubs his hands, making more coin in a day
than another man's whole fortune comes to. I know
one transaction brought him in a thousand gold denars.
Why! if we were anything better than geldings, he

wouldn't be so pleased with himself long. Nowadays
the folks are lions at home, and foxes abroad.

"As for me, I've eaten up my duds, and if the
scarcity goes on, I shall sell my bits of houses. What
is to become of us, if neither gods nor men take pity
on this unhappy city? As I hope for happiness, I
think it's all the gods' doing. For nobody any more
believes heaven to be heaven, nobody keeps fast,
nobody cares one straw for Jupiter, but all men shut
their eyes and count up their own belongings. In
former days the long-robed matrons went barefoot,
with unbound hair and a pure heart, up the hill to
pray Jupiter for rain; and instantly it started raining
bucketfuls,—then or never,—and they all came back
looking like drowned rats. So the gods come stealthy-
footed to our destruction, because we have no piety.
The fields lie idle.—"

"I beseech you," cried Echion, the old-clothes-man,
at this point, "I beseech you, better words! Luck's
for ever changing, as the chawbacon said, when he
lost his brindled hog. If not to-day, then to-morrow;
that's the way the world wags. My word! you couldn't
name a better countryside, if only the inhabitants were
to match. True, we are in low water for the moment,
but we're not the only ones. We must not be so over
particular, the same heaven is over us all. If you lived
anywhere else, you would say pigs ran about here
ready roasted.

"And I tell you, we're going to have a grand show
in three days from now at the festival—none of your
common gangs of gladiators, but most of the chaps

freedmen. Our good Titus has a heart of gold and
a hot head; 'twill be do or die, and no quarter. I'm
in his service, he is no shirker! He'll have the best
of sharp swords and no backing out; bloody butcher's
meat in the middle, for the amphitheatre to feast their
eyes on. And he's got the wherewithal; he was left
thirty million, his father came to a bad end. Suppose
he does spend four hundred thousand or so, his property won't feel it, and his name will live for ever.
He has already got together a lot of poneys, and a
female chariot fighter, and Glyco's factor, who was
caught diverting his mistress. You'll see what a row
the people will have betwixt the jealous husbands and
the happy lovers. Anyhow, Glyco, who's not worth
twopence, condemned his factor to the beasts,—which
was simply betraying his own dishonour. How was
the servant to blame, who was forced to do what he
did? It was she, the pisspot, deserved tossing by the
bull far more than he. But there, if a man can't get at
the donkey's back, he must thrash the donkey's pack.
And how could Glyco ever suppose Hermogenes' girl
should come to any good. He could cut a kite's claws
flying; a snake doesn't father a rope. Glyco! Glyco!
you've paid your price; as long as you live, you're
a marked man,—a brand Hell only can obliterate.
A man's mistakes always come home to roost.

"Why! I can nose out now what a feast Mammaea
is going to give us, two gold denars each for me and
mine. If he does so, I only hope he'll show no favour
whatever to Norbanus. You may rest assured he will
clap on all sail. And in good sooth what has the

other ever done for us? He gave a show of two-penny halfpenny gladiators, such a rickety lot,—blow on them, they'd have fallen flat; and I've seen better bestiarii. He killed his mounted men by torchlight, you might have taken them for dunghill cocks. One was mule-footed, another bandy-legged, while the third, put up to replace a dead man, was a deadhead himself, for he was hamstrung before beginning. The only one to show any spunk was a Thracian, and he only fought when we tarred him on. In the end they all got a sound thrashing; in fact the crowd had cried 'Trice up!' for every one of them, they were obviously such arrant runaways. 'Anyhow I gave you a show,' said he. 'And I applauded,' said I; 'reckon it up, and I gave you more than I got. One good turn deserves another.'

"You look, Agamemnon, as if you were saying to yourself, 'Whatever is that bore driving at?' I talk, because you fellows who can talk, won't talk. You're not of our stuff, and so you laugh at poor men's con-versation. You're a monument of learning, we all know. But there, let me persuade you one day to come down into the country and see our little place. We'll find something to eat, a pullet and a few eggs; it will be grand, even though the bad weather this year has turned everything upside down. Anyway we shall find enough to fill our bellies.

"And there's a future pupil growing up for you, my little lad at home. He can repeat four pieces already; if he lives, you will have a little servant at your beck and call. If he has a spare moment, he

never lifts his head from his slate. He's a bright lad
with good stuff in him, though he is so gone on birds.
I've killed three linnets of his, and told him a weasel
ate 'em. But he has found other hobbies, and he's
devoted to painting. Why! he is already showing his
heels to the Greek, and beginning to take capitally to
his Latin, though his master is too easy going and too
restless; he knows his work well enough, but won't
take proper pains. Then there's another, not a learned
man but a very ingenious one, who teaches more than
he knows. Accordingly he comes to the house on high
days and holidays, and whatever you give him, he
looks pleased. So I've just bought the lad some law
books, for I want him to have a smack of law for
home use. There's bread and butter in that. For as
to Literature, he has been tarred enough already with
that brush. If he kicks, I've made up my mind to
teach him a trade,—a barber, or an auctioneer, or
best of all a lawyer,—which nothing but Hell can
rob him of. So I impress on him every day. 'Believe
me, my first-born, whatever you learn, you learn for
your good. Look at Phileros the advocate; if he
hadn't studied, he would be starving today. The
other day, just the other day, he was carting things
round on his own shoulders, now he is a match for
Norbanus himself. Learning's a treasure, and a trade
never starves.' " Such were the brilliant remarks that
were flashing round the board, when Trimalchio re-
entered, and after wiping his brow and scenting his
hands, "Pardon me, my friends," he said after a brief
pause, "but for several days I have been costive. My

physicians were non-plussed. However, pomegranate
rind and an infusion of fir-wood in vinegar has done
me good. And now I trust my belly will be better
behaved. At times I have such a rumbling about my
stomach, you'd think I had a bull bellowing inside me!
So if any of you want to relieve yourselves, there's no
necessity to be ashamed about it. None of us is born
solid. I don't know any torment so bad as holding
it in. It's the one thing Jove himself cannot stop.
What are you laughing at, Fortunata,—you who so
often keep me awake o' nights yourself? I never
hinder any man at my table from easing himself, and
indeed the doctors forbid our baulking nature. Even
if something more presses, everything's ready outside,
—water, close-stools, and the other little matters needful. Take my word for it, the vapours rise to the
brain and may cause a fluxion of the whole constitu-
tion. I know many a man that's died of it, because
he was too shy to speak out."

We thank our host for his generous indulgence,
taking our wine in little sips the while to keep down
our laughter. But little we thought we had still another hill to climb, as the saying is, and were only half
way through the elaboration of the meal. For when
the tables had been cleared with a flourish of music,
three white hogs were brought in, hung with little bells
and muzzled. One, so the nomenclator informed us,
was a two year old, another three, and the third six.
For my part, I thought they were learned pigs, come in
to perform some of those marvellous tricks you see
in circuses. But Trimalchio put an end to my surmises

by saying, "Which of the three will you have dressed
for supper right away? Farmyard cocks and pheas-
ants and suchlike small deer are for country folks;
my cooks are used to serving up calves boiled whole."

So saying, he immediately ordered the cook to be
summoned, and without waiting for our choice, directed
the six year old to be killed. Then speaking loud and
clear, he asked the man, "What decuria do you belong to?"

"To the fortieth," he replied.

"Bought," he went on, "or born in my house?"

"Neither," returned the cook, "I was left you by
Pansa's will."

"Then mind you serve the dish carefully dressed;
else I shall order you to be degraded into the decuria
of the outdoor slaves."

And the cook, thus cogently admonished, then withdrew with his charge into the kitchen.

But Trimalchio, relaxing his stern aspect, now
turned to us and said, "If you don't like the wine, I'll
have it changed; otherwise please prove its quality by
your drinking. Thanks to the gods' goodness, I never
buy it; but now I have everything that smacks good
growing on a suburban estate of mine. I've not seen
it yet, but they tell me it's down Terracina and Tarentum way. I am thinking at the moment of making
Sicily one of my little properties, that when I've a mind
to visit Africa, I may sail along my own boundaries
to get there.

"But tell me, Agamemnon, what question formed the
subject of your declamation to-day? Though I don't

plead myself, I've studied letters for domestic use. Don't imagine I have despised scholarship; why! I have two Libraries, one Greek, the other Latin. If you love me, then, let me know what the argument of your discourse was."

Agamemnon had just begun, "A poor man and a rich were at feud . . .," when Trimalchio struck in with the question, "What is a poor man!"

"Oh, capital!" cried Agamemnon; and went on to develop some dialectical problem or another.

Trimalchio summed up without an instant's hesitation as follows, "If this is so, there's no question about it; if it's not so, why! there's an end of the matter."

Whilst we were still acclaiming these and similar remarks with fulsome praise, he resumed, "Pray, my dearest Agamemnon, do you recollect by any chance the twelve labours of Hercules, or the story of Ulysses, how the Cyclops twisted his thumb out of joint, after he was turned into a pig. I used to read these tales in Homer when I was a lad. Then the Sibyl! I saw her at Cumae with my own eyes hanging in a jar; and when the boys cried to her, 'Sibyl, what would you?' she would answer, 'I would die,'—both of 'em speaking Greek."

CHAPTER EIGHT

He was still in the middle of this nonsense when a tray supporting an enormous hog was set on the table. One and all we expressed our admiration at the expedition shown, and swore a mere ordinary fowl could not have been cooked in the time,—the more so as the hog appeared to be a much larger animal than the wild boar just before. Presently Trimalchio, staring harder and harder, exclaimed, "What! what! isn't he gutted? No! by heaven! he's not. Call the cook in!"

The cook came and stood by the table, looking sadly crestfallen and saying he had clean forgotten. "What! forgotten!" cried Trimalchio; "to hear him, you would suppose he'd just omitted a pinch of pepper or a bit of cummin. Strip him!"

Instantly the cook was stripped, and standing between two tormentors, the picture of misery. But we all began to intercede for him, saying, "Accidents will happen; do forgive him this once. If ever he does it again, not one of us will say a word in his favour." For my own part I felt mercilessly indignant, and could not hold myself, but bending over to Agamemnon's ear, I whispered, "Evidently he must be a villainous bad servant. To think of anybody forgetting to bowel a hog; by Gad! I would not let the fellow off, if he'd shown such carelessness about a fish."

Not so Trimalchio, for with a smile breaking over his face, "Well! well!" said he, "as you have such a bad memory, bowel him now, where we can all see."

Thereupon the cook resumed his tunic, seized his knife and with a trembling hand slashed open the animal's belly. In a moment, the apertures widening under the weight behind, out tumbled a lot of sausages and black-puddings.

At this all the servants applauded like one man, and chorussed, "Gaius for ever!" Moreover the cook was gratified with a goblet of wine and a silver wreath, and received a drinking cup on a salver of Corinthian metal. This Agamemnon scanned with some attention, and Trimalchio observed, "I am the only man possessing the genuine Corinthian plate."

I fully expected him to match his usual effrontery by declaring he had himself imported the articles from Corinth; but he had a better account to give of the matter. "You may wonder perhaps," he said, "why I alone have the true Corinthian. The fact is, the smith I buy them from is called Corinth, and what can be more Corinthian than to have Corinth at one's orders? But you must not set me down for a dunce; I know perfectly well how Corinthian plate first originated. On the capture of Troy, Hannibal, an astute fellow and a consummate knave, collected together all the statues of bronze and gold and silver into one great heap, and firing the pile, melted down the different metals into one alloy. This mass of metal the smiths utilized to make into platters and dishes and statuettes.

Such was the origin of Corinthian metal,—neither one thing nor the other, but an amalgam of all.

"But you must allow me to say this, I prefer glass ones myself; they are quite free from smell at any rate. And if they didn't break, I would rather have them than gold itself; but they've got cheap and common now. However there was an artificer once who made a glass goblet that would not break. So he was admitted to Caesar's presence to offer him his invention; then, on receiving the cup back from Caesar's hands, he dashed it down on the floor. Who so startled as Caesar? but the man quietly picked up the goblet again, which was dented as a vessel of bronze might be. Then taking a little hammer from his pocket, he easily and neatly knocked the goblet into shape again. This done, the fellow thought he was as good as in heaven already, especially when Caesar said to him, 'Does anybody else besides yourself understand the manufacture of this glass?' But lo! on his replying in the negative, Caesar ordered him to be beheaded, because if once the secret became known, we should think no more of gold than of so much dirt.

"I'm quite a connoisseur in plate. I've got cups as big as waterpots, a hundred of them more or less, representing how Cassandra slew her sons, and there lie the lads dead, as natural as life! I've got a thousand bowls Mummius bequeathed to my patron, on which Daedalus is shown shutting Niobe up in the Trojan horse. Why! I've got the fights of Hermeros and Petraites on a series of cups all of massive metal.

I wouldn't sell my savvy in these things for any money."

In the middle of these remarks a slave dropped a cup. Trimalchio looked at him and said, "Go at once and kill yourself; you are a careless fellow." The slave immediately dropped his lip and began to beg for mercy. "Why worry me," cried Trimalchio, "as if I were being harsh upon you. I merely urge you to secure yourself from being so heedless again." At length, on our entreaty, he pardoned the man. The latter, to celebrate the event, began running round and round the table, crying, "Out water, in wine!" We were all ready to take the merry rascal's kind suggestion, and particularly Agamemnon, who knew very well how to earn another invitation. But Trimalchio under the stimulus of our flattery drank away more gaily than ever, and being close on the verge of intoxication, "Won't any of you," he cried, "ask my wife Fortunata to dance? Believe me, there's no one foots the cancan better." Then putting up his two hands himself above his brow, he began imitating Syrus the comedian, the whole household singing out, "Bravo! Oh, bravissimo!" in chorus; and he would have made a public exhibition of himself, had not Fortunata whispered in his ear and told him, I suppose, that suchlike buffooneries were beneath his dignity. But nothing could well be more uncertain than his humour; one moment he would listen respectfully to Fortunata, the next hark back to his natural propensities.

However, his dancing fit was cut short by the entrance of the Historiographer, who read out solemnly, as if he were reciting the public records:

"Seventh of Kalends of July (June 25.): On the manor of Cumae, Trimalchio's property, were born this day thirty boys, forty girls; were carried from threshing-floor to granary 500,000 bushels of wheat; were put to the yoke 500 oxen.

"Same day: Mithridates, a slave, was crucified for blaspheming our master Gaius' tutelary genius.

"Same day: returned to treasury ten million sesterces, no investment being forthcoming for the sum.

"Same day: a fire occurred in Pompey's gardens, originating at the house of Nasta, the Bailiff."

"Eh?" interrupted Trimalchio, "when were Pompey's gardens bought for me?"

"Last year," answered the Historiographer; "therefore they have not been brought into account yet."

Trimalchio blazed up at this and shouted, "Any estates bought in my name, if I hear nothing of them within six months, I forbid their being carried to my account at all."

Next were read his Ædiles' edict and Foresters' wills, in which Trimalchio was excluded from inheritance, but mentioned with the highest encomiums. Then the names of his Bailiffs were recited; how the Chief Inspector had repudiated his mistress, a freedwoman, having detected her in an intrigue with the Bath-Superintendent; how the Chamberlain had been removed to Baiae; the Steward convicted of peculation; and a dispute between the Grooms of the Chamber adjudicated upon.

But now the acrobats entered at last. A most
tiresome, dull fellow stood supporting a ladder, up
the rungs of which he ordered a lad to climb and dance
and sing on the top, and then leap down through blazing hoops holding a wine-jar in his teeth. Trimalchio
was the only person present who admired this performance, saying it was a hard life truly. There were
but two things, he went on, in all the world he really
enjoyed seeing—acrobats and horn-blowers; all other
shows were mere trash. "Yes! I bought a company of
Comedians too," he said, "but I insisted on their
playing Atellanes, and I ordered my conductor to play
Latin airs and Latin airs only."

In the middle of these fine remarks of the great
Gaius, the boy suddenly tumbled down on top of our
host. The domestics all raised a shriek, and the guests
as well, not for any love they bore the disgusting creature, whose neck they would have gladly seen broken,
but for fear of a bad end to the feast and the necessity
of lamenting the man's death. Trimalchio himself
gave a deep groan and bent over one arm, as if it
were injured. His physicians flocked round him, and
amongst the foremost Fortunata with streaming hair
and a cup in her hand, asseverating she was a miserable, unhappy woman. The boy for his part who had
fallen was already creeping round at our knees, beseeching us to intercede for him. I was tormented
with the idea these prayers were only intended to lead
up by some ridiculous turn to another theatrical de-
nouement. For the cook who had forgotten to bowel
the hog still stuck in my memory. So I began to carry

my eyes all about the room, to see if the wall would
not open to admit some stage-machine or other,—especially after observing how a slave was thrashed, who
had bandaged his master's bruised arm with white
instead of purple wool. Nor was I far out in my
suspicions, for in lieu of punishment being inflicted,
Trimalchio now ruled that the lad must be made free,
that none might be able to say so noble a gentleman
had been injured by a slave. We acclaim the generous
act, and indulge in a string of platitudes on the pre-
cariousness of human affairs. "Well, then!" interposed
Trimalchio, "an accident like this must not be allowed
to pass without an impromptu," and instantly calling
for his tablets, and without much racking of brains,
he read out the following lines:

"When least we think, things go astray,
Dame Fortune o'er our life holds sway;
Then drink, make merry, whilst ye may!"

This epigram led the way to a discussion of poets
and poetry, and for some time the palm of song was
awarded to Mopsus the Thracian, until Trimalchio
remarked to Agamemnon, "Pray, master, what do you
consider the difference to be between Cicero and Pub-
lilius? For my own part, I consider the former the
more eloquent author, the latter the more genteel.
What for instance can be better put than this:

" 'Tis arrant luxury undoes the State;
To please your palate pampered peacocks die,
That flaunt their plumed Assyrian gold abroad
For you Numidian fowl and capon fat.

Even the kindly stork is sacrificed,
Our graceful, noisy, long-legged friend,
Fearful of winter's cold and harbinger of Spring,
And finds the cruel cooking-pot its nest.
Why are the Indian pearls so dear to you,—
If not to deck with sea-sought gems the wife
That lifts a wanton leg adulterously?
Why love you so the emerald's greeny gleam,
And flashing fires of Punic carbuncles?
Honour and virtue are the truest gems.
Is't right the bride should wear the woven wind,
And stand exposed in garments thin as air?"

"Now what do you hold to be the most difficult
calling," he went on, "after Literature? I think the
doctor's and the money-changer's; the doctor, because
he's got to know what chaps have in their insides, and
when the fever's coming,—though truly I hate 'em like
fury, for they're for ever ordering me duck-broth; the
money-changer, who detects the bronze underneath the
surface plating of silver.

"Of beasts the most hard-working are oxen and
sheep; to the former we owe the bread we eat, while
'tis the latter make us so fine with their wool. What
a brutal shame it is when a man eats mutton and wears
a woollen coat! Now bees,—I do think they are God's
own creatures, for they vomit honey, though some
say they bring it down from Jupiter. And that's why
they sting, for you'll never find sweet without sour."

He was still cutting out the philosophers in this
fashion, when lottery tickets were passed round in a

cup, and a slave, whose special duty this was, read out the presents to be distributed in the tombola:

"Humbug Silver; a gammon of bacon was shown, with cruets of that metal standing on it.

A Neck-Pillow; and a neck of mutton was produced.

Forbidden Fruits and Contumely; pommeloes were brought in, and a punt-pole with an apple.

Leeks and Peaches; the drawer received a whip and a knife.

Dress Clothes and Morning Coat; a piece of meat and a memorandum book.

Canal and Foot Measure; a hare and a slipper.

Lamprey and Letter; a mouse and a frog tied together, and a bundle of beet-root."

We laughed loud and long; and there were a hundred and fifty other conceits of the same sort that have escaped my memory.

CHAPTER NINE

BUT Ascyltos, lost to all self-control, threw his arms
up in the air, and turning the whole proceedings into
ridicule, laughed till the tears ran down his cheeks. At
this one of the freedmen among the guests, the same
who occupied the place next above me, lost his temper
and shouted, "What are you laughing at, mutton-
head? Isn't my master's elegant hospitality to your
taste? You're a mighty fine gentleman, I suppose,
and used to better entertainment. So help me the
guardian spirits of this house, but I would have made
him baa to some purpose, had I been next him. A
pretty sprig indeed, to laugh at other people! a vagabond from who knows where, a night-raker, that's not
worth his own piddle! Just let me piss round him,
and he would not know how to save his life! By the
powers, I'm not as a rule quick to take offence, but
there! worms are bred in soft flesh. He's laughing;
what's he got to laugh at? Did his father buy the
brat for money? You're a Roman knight: and I'm
a king's son. 'Why did you serve as a slave then?'
Why! because I chose to, and thought it better to be
a Roman citizen than a tributary king. And hence-
forth I hope to live a life beyond the reach of any
one's ridicule. I am a man now among men; I can
walk about with my nose in the air. I owe nobody a

brass farthing; I've never made composition; no one ever stopped me in the forum with a 'Pay me that thou owest!' I've bought some bits of land, put by a trifle of tin; I keep twenty folks in victuals, to say nothing of the dog; I've purchased my bedfellow's freedom, that no man should wipe his hands on her bosom; I paid a thousand denars to redeem her; I was made a sevir, free gratis for nothing; I trust I may die and have no cause to blush in my grave. But you, are you so busy you can't so much as look behind you? You can spy a louse on a neighbour's back, and never see the great tick on your own. You're the only man to find us ridiculous; there's your master and your elder, he likes us well enough, I warrant. You! with your mammy's milk scarce dry on your lips, you can't say bo! to a goose; you crock, you limp scrap of soaked leather, you may be supple, but you're no good. Are you richer than other folk? then dine twice over, and sup twice! For myself I value my credit far above millions. Did any man ever dun me twice? I served forty years, but nobody knows whether I was slave or free. I was a long-haired lad when first I came to this town; the basilica was not built yet. But I took pains to please my master, a great, grand gentleman and a dignified, whose nail-pairings were worth more than your whole body. And I had enemies in the house, let me tell you, quite ready to trip me up on occasion; but— thanks to his kind nature—I swam the rapids. That's the real struggle; for to be born a gentleman is as easy as 'Come here.' Whatever are you gaping at now, like a buckgoat in a field of bitter vetch?"

At this harangue Giton, who was standing at my feet, could no longer contain himself, but burst into a most indecorous peal of merriment. When Ascyltos' adversary noticed the fact, he turned his abuse upon the lad, screaming, "You're laughing too, are you, you curled onion? Ho! for the Saturnalia, is it December, pray? When did you stump up your twentieth? What's he at now, the crow's meat gallows-bird? I'll take care God's anger falls on you, you and your master who does not keep you in better order. As I hope to live by bread, I only keep my hands off you out of respect for my fellow freedmen; else would I have paid you off this instant minute. We're right enough, but your folks are good for nothing, who don't keep you to heel. Verily, like master like man. I can scarce hold myself, and I'm not a hot-headed man naturally; but if I once begin, I don't care two-pence for my own mother. All right, I shall come across you yet in the open street, you rat, you mushroom, you! I'll never stir up nor down, if I don't drive your master into a wretched hole, and show you what's what, though you call upon Olympian Jove himself to help you! I'll be the ruin of your rubbishy ringlets and your twopenny master into the bargain. All right, see if I don't get my teeth into you; either I don't know myself, or you shall laugh on the wrong side of your face, even if you had a beard of gold. I'll see that Minerva's down on you, and the man that first trained you to be what you are.

"I never learned Geometry and Criticism and such like nonsensical screeds, but I do understand the lapidaries' marks, and I can subdivide to the hundredth part when it comes to questions of mass, and weight and mintage. Well and good! if you have a mind, we'll have a little wager, you and I; come now, here I clap down the tin. You'll soon see your father wasted his money on you, though you do know Rhetoric. Now:

'Which of us?—I come long, I come wide:
   now guess me.'

"I'll tell you which of us runs, yet never stirs from the spot; which of us grows, and gets less all the while. How you skip and fidget and fuss, like a mouse in a chamber-pot! So either hold your tongue altogether, or don't attack a better man than yourself, who hardly knows of your existence,—unless perhaps you think I'm troubled by your yellow ringlets, that you stole from your doxy. God helps the man that helps himself! Let's away to the forum to borrow money; you'll soon see this bit of iron commands some credit. Aha! a fine sight, a fox in a sweat! As I hope to thrive and make such a good end the people will all be swearing at my death, hang me if I don't chivy you up hill and down dale till you drop! A fine sight too, the fellow that taught you so,—a muff I call him, not a master! We learned something else in my time; the master used to say, 'Are your things safe? go straight home; don't stop staring about, and don't be impertinent to your elders.' Now it's all trash; they turn out nobody worth twopence. That I am what I am, I owe to my own wits, and I thank God for it!"

Ascyltos was just beginning to answer his abuse; but
Trimalchio, charmed with his fellow-freedman's eloquence, stopped him, saying, "Come, come! leave your
bickerings on one side. Better be good-natured; and
do you, Hermeros, spare the young man. His blood
is up; so be reasonable. To yield is always to win in
these matters. You were a young cockerel yourself
once, and then coco coco you went, and never a grain
of sense in you! So take my advice, let's start afresh
and be jolly, while we enjoy the Homerists."

Immediately there filed in an armed band, and
clashed spears on shields. Trimalchio himself sat in
state on his cushion, and when the Homerists began
a dialogue in Greek verse, as is their unmannerly manner, read out a Latin text in a clear, loud voice. Presently in an interval of silence, "You know," says he,
"what is the tale they are giving us?" Diomed and
Ganymede were two brothers. Their sister was Helen
of Troy. Agamemnon carried her off and palmed a
doe on Diana in her stead. So Homer relates how
the Trojans and Parantines fought each other. He
got the best of it, it seems, and gave his daughter
Iphigenia in marriage to Achilles. This drove Ajax
mad, who will presently make it all plain to you."
No sooner had Trimalchio finished speaking than the
Homerists raised a shout, and with the servants bustling in all directions, a boiled calf was borne in on
a silver dish weighing two hundred pounds, and actually wearing a helmet. Then came Ajax, and rushing
at it like a madman slashed it to bits with his naked
sword, and making passes now up and down, collected

the pieces on his point and so distributed the flesh among the astonished guests.

We had little time however to admire these elegant surprises; for all of a sudden the ceiling began to rattle and the whole room trembled. I sprang up in consternation, fearing some tumbler was going to fall through the roof. The other guests were no less astounded, and gazed aloft, wondering what new prodigy they were to expect now from the skies. Then lo and behold! the ceiling opened and a huge hoop, evidently stripped from an enormous cask, was let down, all around which hung suspended golden wreaths and caskets containing precious unguents. These we were invited to take home with us as mementos.

Then looking again at the table, I saw that a tray of cakes had been placed on it, with a figure of Priapus, the handiwork of the pastry-cook, standing in the middle, represented in the conventional way as carry-ing in his capacious bosom grapes and all sorts of fruits. Eagerly we reached out after these dainties, when instantly a new sell set us laughing afresh. For each cake and each fruit was full of saffron, which spurted out into our faces at the slightest touch, giving us an unpleasant drenching. So conceiving there must be something specially holy about this dish, scented as it was in this ceremonial fashion, we rose to our feet, crying, "All hail, Augustus, Father of his Country!" But seeing the others still helping themselves to the dessert, even after this act of piety, we also filled our napkins,—myself among the foremost, as I thought no gift good enough to pour into my beloved Giton's bosom. Meantime three slaves entered wearing short white jackets. Two of them set on the table images of the Lares with amulets round their necks, while the third carried round a goblet of wine, crying, "The gods be favourable! the gods be favourable!" Trimalchio told us they were named respectively Cerdo, Felicio and Lucrio. Then came a faithful likeness of Trimalchio in marble, and as everybody else kissed it, we were ashamed not to do likewise.

Then after we had all wished one another good health of mind and body, Trimalchio turned to Niceros and said, "You used to be better company; what makes you so dull and silent to-day? I beg you, if you wish to oblige me, tell us that adventure of yours." Niceros, delighted at his friend's affability, replied, "May I never make profit more, if I'm not ready to burst with satisfaction to see you so well disposed, Trimalchio. So, ho! for a pleasant hour,—though I very much fear these learned chaps will laugh at me. Well, let 'em. I'll say my say for all that! What does it hurt me, if a man does grin? Better they should laugh with me than at me." "These words the hero spake," and so began the following strange story:

"When I was still a slave, we lived in a narrow street; the house is Gavilla's now. There, as the gods would have it, I fell in love with Terentius the tavern-keeper's wife; you all knew Melissa from Tarentum, the prettiest of pretty wenches! Not that I courted her carnally or for venery, but more because she was such a good sort. Nothing I asked did she ever refuse; if she made a penny, I got a halfpenny; whatever I saved, I put in her purse, and she never choused me. Well! her husband died when they were at a country house. So I moved heaven and earth to get to her; true friends, you know, are proved in adversity.

"It so happened my master had gone to Capua, to attend to various trifles of business. So seizing the opportunity, I persuaded our lodger to accompany me as far as the fifth milestone. He was a soldier, as bold as Hell. We got under weigh about first cockcrow, the moon shining as bright as day. We arrive at the tombs; my man lingers behind among the gravestones, while I sit down singing, and start counting the grave-stones. Presently I looked back for my comrade; he had stripped off all his clothes and laid them down by the wayside. My heart was in my mouth; and there I stood feeling like a dead man. Then he made water all round the clothes, and in an instant changed into a wolf. Don't imagine I'm joking; I would not tell a lie for the finest fortune ever man had.

"However, as I was telling you, directly he was turned into a wolf, he set up a howl, and away to the woods. At first I didn't know where I was, but presently I went forward to gather up his clothes; but lo and behold! they were turned into stone. If ever a man was like to die of terror, I was that man! Still I drew my sword and let out at every shadow on the road, till I arrived at my sweetheart's house. I rushed in looking like a ghost, soul and body barely sticking together. The sweat was pouring down between my legs, my eyes were set, my wits gone almost past recovery. Melissa was astounded at my plight, wondering why ever I was abroad so late. 'Had you come a little sooner,' she said, 'you might have given us a hand; a wolf broke into the farm and has slaughtered all the cattle, just as if a butcher had bled them. Still he didn't altogether have the laugh of us, though he did escape; for one of the labourers ran him through the neck with a pike.'

"After hearing this, I could not close an eye, but directly it was broad daylight, I started off for our good Gaius's house, like a pedlar whose pack's been stolen; and coming to the spot where the clothes had been turned into stone, I found nothing whatever but a pool of blood. When eventually I got home, there lay my soldier a-bed like a great ox, while a surgeon was dressing his neck. I saw at once he was a were-wolf and I could never afterwards eat bread with him, no! not if you'd killed me. Other people may think what they please; but as for me, if I'm telling you a lie, may your guardian spirits confound me!"

We were all struck dumb with amazement, till Tri-malchio broke the silence, saying, "Far be it from me to doubt your story; if you'll believe me, my hair stood on end, for I know Niceros is not the man to repeat idle fables; he's perfectly trustworthy and anything but a babbler. Now! I'll tell you a horrible tale my-self, as much out of the common as an ass on the tiles!

"I was still but a long-haired lad (for I led a Chian life from a boy) when our master's minion died,—a pearl, by heaven! a paragon of perfection at all points. Well! as his poor mother was mourning him, and several of us besides condoling with her, all of a sudden the witches set up their hullabaloo, for all the world like a hound in full cry after a hare. At that time we had a Cappadocian in the household, a tall fellow, and a high-spirited, and strong enough to lift a mad bull off its feet. This man gallantly drawing his sword dashed out in front of the house door, first winding his cloak carefully round his left arm, and lunging out, as it might be there—no harm to what I touch—ran a woman clean through. We heard a grown, but the actual witches (I'm very particular to tell the exact truth) we did not see. Coming in again, our champion threw himself down on a bed, and his body was black and blue all over, just as if he had been scourged with whips, for it seems an evil hand had touched him. We barred the door and turned back afresh to our lamentations, but when his mother threw her arms round her boy and touched his dead body, she found nothing but a wisp of straw. It had neither heart, nor entrails, nor anything else; for the witches had whipped away the lad and left a changeling of straw in his place. Now I ask you, can you help after this believing there are wise women, hags that fly by night, and what's more, that can turn the world upside down? But our tall bully, after what happened then, never got back his colour, in fact a few days afterward he died raving mad!"

We listened with wonder and credulity in equal proportions, and kissing the table, besought the Night-hags to keep in quarters, while we were returning home after our dinner.

And indeed by this time the lights seemed to burn

double and I thought the whole room looked changed, when Trimalchio exclaimed, "I call on you, Plocamus; have you nothing to tell us? no diversion for us? And you used to be such good company, with your amusing dialogues and the comic songs you interspersed. Heigho! all gone ye toothsome titbits, all gone?" "Alas! my racing days are over, since I got the gout," replied the other; "but when I was a young man, I very nearly sang myself into a consumption. Dancing? dialogues? buffoonery? when did I ever find my match, eh?—always excepting Apelles." And clapping his hand to his mouth, he spit out some horrid stuff that sounded like whistling, and which he told us afterwards was Greek.

Moreover Trimalchio himself gave an imitation of a horn-blower, and presently turned to his minion whom he called Crœsus. This was a lad with sore eyes and filthy teeth: he was playing with a little black bitch, disgustingly fat, twisting a green scarf round her, putting half a loaf of bread on the couch, and on the animal's refusing to eat it, being already overfed, cramming it down her throat. This reminding Trimalchio of a duty omitted, he ordered Scylax to be brought in, "the guardian of my house and home." Next moment a huge watch-dog was led in on a chain, and being admonished by a kick from the porter to lie down, took up a position in front of the table. Then Trimalchio tossed him a lump of white bread, observing, "There's no one in the house loves me better." The boy was enraged at hearing Scylax so lavishly praised, and setting his bitch down on the floor, cheered her on to attack the monster. Scylax, as was his nature to, filled the room with savage barking, and almost tore Crœsus's little "Pearl" into bits. Nor was the fight the end of the trouble; but a chandelier was upset over the table, smashing all the crystals, and bespattering some of the guests with scalding oil.

Trimalchio, not to appear disconcerted at the damage done, kissed the lad and told him to get up on his back. The latter mounted a-cockhorse without a moment's hesitation, and repeatedly slapping him on the shoulders with his open hand, laughingly shouted, "Buck! buck! how many fingers do I hold up?" After thus submitting for a while to be made a horse of, Trimalchio ordered them to prepare a capacious bowl of wine and give drinks to all the slaves sitting at our feet, but on this condition, he added, "If anyone won't take his whack, souse it over his head! Business in the day time, now for jollity!"

CHAPTER TEN

AFTER this display of good-nature, there followed a course of delicacies, only to think of which, if you'll believe me, makes me feel ill. For instead of thrushes, a fatted hen was set before each guest and chaperoned goose-eggs which Trimalchio urged us most pressingly to partake of, assuring us the hens were boned.

At this moment a lictor knocked at the folding doors of the dining-hall, and dressed out in a white robe, a fresh boon-companion now entered with a large train in attendance. As for me, I was so much impressed by all this state and ceremony, I thought it was the Praetor. So I made as if to rise and set my naked feet to the floor. Agamemnon laughed at my trepidation; "Sit still, you silly fellow," said he, "it's Habinnas the Sevir, he's a marble-mason, and it seems makes capital good monuments." Reassured by what he said, I lay back again in my place, and watched Habinnas' entry with the greatest admiration. He was already tipsy, and leant for support on his wife's shoulder; wearing several heavy wreaths round his brow, which was so reeking with perfume it kept trickling into his eyes, he took the Praetor's place, and at once called for wine and hot water.

Delighted at his joviality, Trimalchio himself called for a large goblet, and asked him how he had been entertained. "We had everything in the world," he replied, "except the pleasure of your company; for indeed my inclinations were here. But upon my word, it was very fine. Scissa was giving a very elegant novendial in memory of her poor old slave, whom she had enfranchised after his death. And I suppose she will have a good round sum to pay to the tax-collectors, for they do tell me the dead man's fortune came to fifty thousand. I assure you it was all very pleasant, though we did have to pour half our liquor over his old bones."

"But what did you have for dinner?" Trimalchio asked.

"I'll tell you, if I can," was the answer, "but there, I have such a first-class memory, I often forget my own name. However, for first course we had a pig topped with a black-pudding and garnished with fritters and giblets, capitally dressed, and beetroot of course, and whole-meal brown bread, which I prefer myself to white; it makes muscle, and when I do my does, I don't have to yell. The next course was cold tarts, and to drink, excellent Spanish wine poured over warm honey. So I ate a fine helping of tart, and smeared myself well with the honey. As accessories, were chick-peas and lupins, nuts at discretion, and an apple apiece. But I took two, and look you! I've got them here tied up in a napkin; for if I don't take some present back for my little slave lad at home, there'll be a row. Right! my wife reminds me, we had also, on the sideboard a joint of bear's meat. Scintilla took some inadvertently, and very nearly threw up her guts. I on the contrary ate nearly a pound of it; indeed it tasted quite like

boar's flesh. And what I say is, if bear eats man, why
should not man, with a far better reason, eat bear?
To end up with, we had cream cheese flavoured with
wine jelly, snails, one apiece, chitterlings, scalloped
liver and chaperonned eggs, turnips, mustard and (by
your leave, Palamedes!) a dish of mixed siftings;
pickled olives also were handed round in a bowl, from
which some of the party were mean enough to help
themselves to three handfuls each; the ham we declined
altogether.

"But pray, Gaius, why is not Fortunata at table?"

"Don't you know her better than that?" answered
Trimalchio. "Not until she has counted the plate, and
divided the leavings among the slaves, will she let so
much as a drop of water pass her lips."

"Well!" returned Habinnas, "if she does not join
us, I'm off, for one;" and made as though to get up.
when at a signal from their master the whole house-
full of slaves called out, four times over and more,
"Fortunata! Fortunata!" At this she entered at last,
her frock kilted up with a yellow girdle, so as to show a
cherry-coloured tunic underneath, and corded anklets
and gold-embroidered slippers. Then wiping her hands
on a handkerchief she wore at her neck, she placed
herself on the same couch beside Habinnas' wife,
Scintilla, kissing her while the other claps her hands,
and exclaiming, "Have I really the pleasure of seeing
you?"

Before long it came to Fortunata's taking off the
blacelets from her great fat arms to show them to
her admiring companion. Finally she even undid her

anklets and her hairnet, which she assured Scintilla
was of the very finest gold. Trimalchio observing this,
ordered all the things to be brought to him. "You see
this woman's fetters," he cried; "that's the way we
poor devils are robbed! Six pounds and a half, if it's
an ounce, and yet I've got one myself of ten pounds
weight, all made out of Mercury's thousandths."
Eventually to prove he was not telling a lie, he ordered
a pair of scales to be brought, and had the articles
carried round and the weight tested by each in turn.
And Scintilla was just as bad, for she drew from her
bosom a little gold casket she called her Lucky Box.
From it she produced a pair of ear-pendants and
handed them one after the other to Fortunata to
admire, saying, "Thanks to my husband's goodness,
no wife has finer."

"Why truly!" remarked Habinnas, "you gave me
no peace till I bought you the glass bean. I tell you
straight, if I had a daughter, I should cut off her ears.
If there were no women in the world, we should have
everything in the world dirt cheap; as it is, we've just
got to piss hot and drink cold."

Meanwhile the two women, though a trifle piqued,
laughed good-humouredly together and interchanged
some tipsy kisses, the one praising the thrifty manage-
ment of the lady of the house, the other enlarging on
the minions her husband kept and his unthrifty ways.
While they were thus engaged in close confabulation,
Habinnas got up stealthily and catching hold of Fortunata's legs, upset her on the couch. "Ah! ah!" she
screeched, as her tunic slipped up above her knees.

Then falling on Scintilla's bosom, she hid in her handkerchief a face all afire with blushes.

After a short interval Trimalchio next ordered the
dessert to be served; hereupon the servants removed
all the tables and brought in fresh ones, and strewed
the floor with saffron and vermilion coloured saw-dust
and,—a refinement I had not seen before,—with specu-
lar stone reduced to powder. The moment the tables
were changed, Trimalchio remarked, "I could really
be quite content with what we have; for you see your
'second tables' before you. However, if there is anything spicy for dessert, let's have it in."

Meantime an Alexandrian lad, who served round the
hot water, began imitating a nightingale, his master
from time to time calling out, "Change!" Another
form of entertainment followed. A slave who was
sitting at Habinnas' feet, at his master's bidding, as I
imagine, suddenly sang out in a loud voice:

"Meantime Æneas cuts his watery way. . . ."

Nothing harsher ever shocked my ears, for to say
nothing of the false inflections, now high now low, of
his voice and his barbarous pronunciation, he kept
sticking in tags from Atellane farces, so that for the
first time in my life I found Virgil intolerable. Yet
no sooner did he pause for an instant than Habinnas
loudly applauded the performance, adding, "The man
has had no regular training; I merely sent him to see
some mountebanks, and that's how he learned. The
result is, he has not his match, whether it's muleteers
or mountebanks he wants to mimic. He's just desperate clever; he's cobbler, cook, confectioner, a com-

pendium of all the talents. Still he has two faults, but
for which he would be a perfect paragon: he is cir-
cumcised and he snores. For his squinting, I don't
mind that; Venus has the same little defect. That's
why his tongue is never still, because one eye is pretty
much always on the alert. I gave three hundred denars
for him."

Here Scintilla interrupted the speaker; "You take
good care," she said, "not to mention all the scamp's
qualifications. He's an arrant go-between; but I'll see
to it he has his brand before long."

Trimalchio only laughed and said, "I see he's a
true Cappadocian; always looks out for number one.
And, my word! I don't blame him; for indeed, once
dead, this is a thing nobody can secure us. And you,
Scintilla, don't be so jealous! Believe me, we understand you women. As I hope to be safe and sound,
I used myself to poke her ladyship, so that even my
master got suspicious; and that's why he sent me off
to be factor in the country. But hush, tongue, and
I'll give thee a cake."

Taking everything that was said for high praise,
the foul slave now drew an earthenware lamp from
his bosom, and for more than half an hour mimicked
a trumpeter, while Habinnas accompanied him, squeez-
ing his lip down with his fingers. Finally he actually
stepped out into the middle of the room, and first
imitated a fluteplayer by means of broken reeds; then
with riding-cloak and whip, acted the muleteer, till
Habinnas called him to his side and kissed him, gave

him a drink and cried, "Bravo! Massa, bravo! I'll give you a pair of boots."

We should never have seen the end of these tiresome inflictions but for the Extra-Course now coming in,—thrushes of pastry, stuffed with rasins and walnuts, followed by quinces stuck over with thorns, to represent sea-urchins. This would have been tolerable enough, had it not been for a still more outlandish dish—such a horrible concoction, we would rather have died than touch it. Directly it was on the table, —to all appearance a fatted goose, with fish and fowl of all kinds round it, "Friends," cried Trimalchio, "every single thing you see on that dish is made out of one substance." With my wonted perspicacity, I instantly guessed its nature, and said, giving Agamemnon a look, "For my own part, I shall be greatly surprised, if it is not all made of filth, or at any rate mud. When I was in Rome at the Saturnalia, I saw some sham eatables of the same sort." I had not done speaking when Trimalchio explained, "As I hope to grow a bigger man,—in fortune I mean, not fat,—I declare my cook made it every bit out of a pig. Never was a more invaluable fellow! Give the word, he'll make you a fish of the paunch, a wood-pigeon of the lard, a turtle-dove of the forehand, and a hen of the hind leg! And that's why I very cleverly gave him such a fine and fitting name as Dædalus. And because he's such a good servant, I brought him a present from Rome, a set of knives of Noric steel." These he immediately ordered to be brought in, and examined and admired them, even allowing us to try their edge on our cheeks.

All of a sudden in rushed two slaves, as if fresh from a quarrel at the fountain; at any rate they still had their water-pots hanging from the shoulder-yokes. Then when Trimalchio gave judgment upon their difference, they would neither of them accept his decision, but each smashed the other's pot with a stick. We were horror-struck at the drunken scoundrels' insolence, and looking hard at the combatants, we noticed oysters and scallops tumbling out of the broken pitchers, which another slave gathered up and handed round on a platter. This refinement was matched by the ingenious cook, who now brought in snails on a little silver gridiron, singing the while in a quavering, horribly rasping voice.

I am really ashamed to relate what followed, it was so unheard of a piece of luxury. Long-haired slave boys brought in an unguent in a silver basin, and anointed our feet with it as we lay at table, after first wreathing our legs and ankles with garlands. Afterwards a small quantity of the same perfume was poured into the wine-jars and the lamps.

By this time a strong wish to dance had seized upon Fortunata, while Scintilla's hands were going quicker in applause even than her tongue in chatter, when Trimalchio said, "I give you my permission, Philargyrus, and you, Cario, notorious champion though you are of the green, to take your places at table; also bid Menophila, your bed-fellow, to do the same." To make a long story short, we were all but thrust off

our couches, such a throng of domestics now invaded
the dinner-table. I actually noticed occupying a place
above my own the cook who had made a goose out of
a pig, reeking as he was with fish-pickle and sauces.
Indeed he was not satisfied with merely being present,
but immediately began an imitation of Ephesus the
Tragedian, after which he offered his master a bet
that at the next races the green would score first prize.

Delighted at the challenge, Trimalchio cried, "Yes!
my friends, slaves are human beings too, and have
sucked mother's milk as well as we, though untoward
Circumstance has borne them down. Yet, without
prejudicing me, they shall some day soon drink the
water of the free. In a word, I enfranchise them all
in my will. I bequeath into the bargain a farm and
his bed-fellow to Philargyrus, a street block to Cario,
besides a twentieth and a bed and bedding. I name
Fortunata my heir, and commend her to all my friends'
kindness. And all this I make public, to the end my
whole household may love me now as well as if I were
dead already."

All began to express their gratitude to so kind a
master, when Trimalchio, quite dropping his trifling
vein, ordered a copy of his will to be fetched, and read
it through from beginning to end amid the groans of
all members of the household. Then turning to Habinnas, he asked him, "What say you, dear friend? are
you building my monument according to my directions?
I ask you particularly that at the feet of my effigy you
have my little bitch put, and garlands and perfume
caskets and all Petraites' fights, that by your good

help I may live on even after death. The frontage
is to be a hundred feet long, and it must reach back
two hundred. For I wish to have all kinds of fruit
trees growing around my ashes and plenty of vines.
Surely it's a great mistake to make houses so fine for
the living, yet to give never a thought to these where
we have to dwell, far, far longer. And that's why I
especially insist on the notice:

THIS MONUMENT DOES NOT DESCEND
TO THE HEIR

But I shall take good care to provide in my will
against my remains being insulted. For I intend to
put one of my freedmen in charge of my burial place,
to see the rabble don't come running and shitting up
against my monument. I beg you to have ships under
full sail carved on it, and me sitting on the tribunal, in
my Senator's robes, with five gold rings on my fingers,
and showering money from a bag among the public;
for you remember I gave a public banquet once, two
denars a head. Also there should be shown, if you
approve, a banqueting-hall, and all the people enjoying themselves pleasantly. On my right hand put a
figure of my wife, Fortunata, holding a dove and leading a little bitch on a leash, also my little lad, and some
good capacious wine-jars, stoppered so that the wine
may not escape. Also you may carve a broken urn,
and a boy weeping over it. Also a horologe in the
centre, so that anyone looking to see the time must
willy nilly read my name. As for the lettering, look

this over carefully and see if you think it is good
enough:

HERE LIES
C. POMPEIUS TRIMALCHIO,
A SECOND MAECENAS.
HE WAS NOMINATED SEVIR
IN HIS ABSENCE.
HE MIGHT HAVE BEEN A MEMBER
OF EVERY DECURIA IN ROME,
BUT DECLINED.
PIOUS, BRAVE, HONOURABLE,
HE ROSE FROM THE RANKS.
WITHOUT LEARNING OR EDUCATION,
HE LEFT A MILLION OF MONEY
BEHIND HIM.
FAREWELL;
GO AND DO THOU LIKEWISE!"

When he had finished reading this document, Trimalchio fell to weeping copiously. Fortunata wept
too; so did Habinnas; so did the servants; in fact,
the whole household filled the room with lamentations,
for all the world like guests at a funeral. Indeed I
was beginning to weep myself, when Trimalchio resumed; "Well!" said he, "as we know we've got to
die, why not make the most of life? As I should
like to see you all happy, let's jump into the bath. I
guarantee you'll be none the worse; it's as hot as an
oven."

"Right! right!" cried Habinnas, "to make two days
out of one; nothing I should like better," and springing

up barefoot as he was, he followed Trimalchio, who led the way, clapping his hands.

For myself I said, turning to Ascyltos, "What think you, Ascyltos? as for me, to look at a bath now would kill me."

"Let's consent," he replied; "and then, as they are making for the bathroom, escape in the confusion."

This being agreed upon, Giton led the way through the colonnade, and we reached the house-door, where the watch-dog greeted us with such furious barking that Ascyltos tumbled into the tank in sheer terror. I too, tipsy as I was, and having been once already scared at a painted dog, got dragged in myself in helping him out of the water. However the hall-keeper rescued us, who interfered and quieted the dog, and pulled us out shivering onto terra firma. Giton had already discovered an ingenious way of disarming the animal; anything we had given him from our dinner, he threw to the barking brute, whose temper was appeased and his attention deverted by the food. But when, cold and wet, we asked the hall-keeper to let us out, "You're much mistaken," said he, "if you think you can go out the same way you came in. No guest is ever dismissed by the same door; they enter by one, go out by another."

So what were we poor unfortunates to do now, prisoners in this new kind of labyrinth, and reduced to choose the bath as the only alternative? We took the bull by the horns therefore, and asked the hall-keeper to show us the way there; then throwing off our clothes, which Giton proceeded to dry in the porch, we entered the bath, which we found to be a narrow chamber, more like a cooling cistern than anything else, with Trimalchio standing upright in it. Not even under these circumstances could he refrain from his loathsome trick of boasting, declaring there was nothing more agreeable than to be free of a crowd in bathing, and that his bath-house occupied the exact site of a former bakery. Presently, feeling tired, he sat down, and tempted by the resonance of the bathroom, turned up his tipsy face and open mouth to the vault, and began murdering some of Menecrates' songs, as we were told by those who could make out the words.

The remainder of the company were running hand in hand round the edge of the bath, laughing and shouting at the top of their voices. Others with their hands tied behind their backs, were trying to pick up rings from the pavement in their mouths, or kneeling down, to bend back and kiss the points of their toes. Whilst the others were engaged in these amusements, we got down into the bath, that was being heated for Trimalchio.

After dissipating the fumes of wine by these means, we were next conducted to another dinner-hall, where Fortunata had laid out a dainty banquet of her own. I noticed especially lamps suspended over the table with miniature figures of fishermen in bronze, tables of solid silver, cups of gilt pottery ware round the board, and wine pouring from a wine-skin before our eyes.

Presently Trimalchio said, "You see, friends, a slave of mine has cut his first beard to-day, a very careful, thrifty young man, if I may say so without offence. So let's be jovial, and keep it up till daylight doth appear." Just as he uttered these words, a cock crew. Trimalchio, must disquieted at the circumstance, ordered wine to be poured under the table, and some even to be sprinkled over the lamp; moreover he shifted a ring from his left hand to his right, saying, " 'Tis not for nothing chanticleer has sounded his note of warning; a fire is bound to happen, or some one's going to die in the vicinity. Save us from ill! Anyone bringing me yonder prophet of evil, shall have a present for his pains." No sooner said than done; a cock was instantly produced from somewhere near, which Trimalchio ordered to be killed and put in the pot to boil. He was cut up accordingly by the same clever cordon bleu who a while before had manufactured game and fish out of a pig, and thrown into a stew-pan. Then whilst Dædalus kept the pot boiling, Fortunata ground pepper in a box-wood mill.

These dainties being dispatched, Trimalchio turned to the servants, saying, "What! haven't you had your dinners yet? be off now, and let the relay take your places." Hereupon a second set of attendants came in, the outgoing slaves crying, "Farewell, Gaius!" and the incoming, "Hail, Gaius!" At this point our mirth was disturbed for the first time; for a rather good-looking slave boy having entered along with the new lot of domestics, Trimalchio laid hold of him and started kissing him over and over again. At this Fortunata, to assert "her lawful and equitable rights" (as she put it), began abusing her husband, calling bim an abomination and a disgrace, that he could not restrain his filthy passions, ending up with the epithet "dog!" Trimalchio for his part was so enraged at her railing that he hurled a winecup in his wife's face. Fortunata screamed out, as if she had lost an eye, and clapped her trembling hands to her countenance. Scintilla was equally alarmed, and sheltered her shuddering friend in her bosom. At the same time an officious attendant applied a pitcher of cold water to her cheek, over which the poor lady drooped and fell a-sighing and a-sobbing.

But Trimalchio went on. "What! what!" he stormed, "has the trollop no memory? didn't I take her from the stand in the slave-market, and make her a free woman among her equals? But there, she puffs herself out, like the frog in the fable; she's too proud to spit in her own bosom, the blockhead. If you are born in a hovel, you shouldn't dream of a palace. As I hope to prosper, I'll see to it this Cassandra of the camp is brought to reason. Why! when I was only worth twopence, I might have married ten millions of money. You know I might. Agatho, perfumer to the lady next door, drew me aside, and 'I'll give you a hint,' said he; 'don't let your race die out.' But I with my silly good-nature, and not wanting to seem fickle-minded, I've driven my axe into my own leg. All right! I'll make you long yet to dig me up again with your fingernails! And to show this minute the harm you've done yourself, I forbid you, Habinnas, to put her statue on my tomb at all, that I may not have any scolding when I'm gone. I'll teach her I can do her a mischief; I won't have her so much as kiss my dead body!"

After this thunder-clap, Habinnas began to entreat him to forget and forgive. "Nobody," he urged, "but goes wrong sometimes; we're men after all, not gods." Scintilla spoke to the same purpose with tears in her eyes, and besought him in the name of his good Genius and addressing him as Gaius, to be pacified. Trimalchio could restrain his tears no longer, but cried, "As you hope, Habinnas, to enjoy your little fortune,—if I've done anything wrong, spit in my face. I kissed the good, careful lad, not because he's a pretty boy, but because he's so thrifty and clever. I tell you he can recite ten pieces, reads his book at sight, has bought himself a Thracian costume out of his daily rations, besides an arm-chair and a pair of cups. Does he not deserve to be the apple of my eye? But Fortunata won't have it. That's your pleasure, is it, you tipsy wench? I warn you, make the most of what you've got, your cormorant; and don't make me nasty, sweetheart, else you'll get a taste of my temper. You know me; once I've made up my mind, I'm just as hard as nails!

"However, not to forget the living, pray, my good friends, enjoy yourselves. I was once what you are now, but my own merits have made me what you see. It's gumption makes a man, all the rest's trash. 'Buy cheap, and sell dear,' that's me; one man will tell you one thing, another another, but I'm just bursting with success. What! crying still, grunty pig? Mark me, I'll give you something worth crying for. But as I was

saying, it was my thriftiness raised me to my present
position. When first I came from Asia, I was no higher
than this candlestick. I tell you, I used to measure
myself by it every day; and the sooner to get a beard
under my nose, I would smear my lips with the lamp
oil. But I was my master's joy for fourteen years;
there's nothing disgraceful in doing your master's
bidding. And I satisfied my mistress into the bargain.
You know what I mean; I say no more, for I'm none
of your boasters.

"Eventually, it so pleased the gods, I found myself
king of the castle, and behold! I could twist my master
round my finger. To make a long story short, he
made me co-heir with the Emperor, and I came into
a senatorial fortune. Still no one is ever satisfied.
I longed to be a merchant prince. So, not to be tedious, I built five ships, loaded up with wine,—it was
worth its weight in gold just then,—and sent them off
to Rome. You might have supposed I'd ordered it
so! if you'll believe me, every one of the ships foun-
dered, and that's a fact. In one day Neptune swallowed me up thirty millions. Do you imagine I gave
in? Not I, by my faith! the loss only whetted my
appetite, as if it were a mere nothing. I built more
ships, bigger and better found and luckier, till every
one allowed I was a well-plucked one. Nothing venture, nothing win, you know; and a big ship's a big
venture. I loaded up again with wine, bacon, beans,
perfumery and slaves. Fortunata was a real good wife
to me that time; she sold all her jewelry and all her
clothes, and laid a hundred gold pieces in my hand;

and it proved the leaven of my little property. A thing's soon done, when the gods will it. One voyage I cleared a round ten millions. Instantly I bought back all the farms that had been my late master's; I built a house; I buy up cattle to sell again. Whatever I touched, grew like a honeycomb. When I found I had as large an income as the whole revenue of my native land amounted to, off hands; I withdrew from commerce, and started lending money among freedmen. Moreover, just when I'd quite made up my mind to have no more to do with trade, an astrologer advised me to the same course, a little Greek fellow, that happened to come to our own town, Serapa he was called, up to all the secrets of the gods. He told me things I had clean forgotten, explaining it all as pat as needle and thread; he knew my inside, he could all but tell me what I'd had for dinner the day before. You would have thought he had lived with me all my life.

"Now tell me, Habinnas,—you were there at the time, I think—didn't he say: 'You have used your wealth to set a mistress over you. You are not very lucky in your friends. No one is ever properly grateful to you. You have enormous estates. You are nourishing a viper beneath your wing?' and—why should I not tell you?—that I have now left me to live thirty years, four months and two days. Also I am soon to come in for another fortune. This is what my Fate has in store for me. And if I have the luck to extend my lands to Apulia, I shall have done pretty well in my day. Meantime by Mercury's good help, I have built this house. You remember it as a cottage; it's as big as a temple now. It has four dining-rooms, twenty bedrooms, two marble porticoes, a series of store-rooms up stairs, the chamber where I sleep myself, this viper's sitting-room, an excellent porter's lodge; while the guest chambers afford ample accommodations. In fact, when Scaurus comes this way, there's nowhere he better likes to stop at, and he has an ancestral mansion of his own by the seaside. Yes! and there are plenty more fine things I'll show you directly. Take my word for it,—Have a penny, good for a penny; Have something, and you're thought something. So your humble servant, who was a toad once upon a time, is a king now.

"Meantime, Stichus, just bring out the grave-clothes I propose to be buried in; also the unguent, and a taste of the wine I wish to have my bones washed with."

Without a moment's delay, Stichus produced a white shroud and a magistrate's gown into the dining-hall, and asked us to feel if they were made of good wool. Then his master added with a laugh, "Mind, Stichus, mice and moth don't get at them; else I'll have you burned alive. I wish to be buried in all my bravery, that the whole people may call down blessings on my head." Immediately afterwards he opened a pot of spikenard, and after rubbing us all with the ointment, "I only hope," said he, "it will give me as much pleasure when I'm dead as it does now when I'm alive." Further he ordered the wine vessels to be filled up, telling us to "imagine you are invited guests at my funeral feast."

The thing was getting positively sickening, when Trimalchio, now in a state of disgusting intoxication, commanded a new diversion, a company of horn-blowers, to be introduced; and then stretching himself out along the edge of a couch on a pile of pillows, "Make believe I am dead," he ordered. "Play something fine." Then the horn-blowers struck up a loud funeral dirge. In particular one of these undertaker's men, the most conscientious of the lot, blew so tremendous a fanfare he roused the whole neighbourhood. Hereupon the watchmen in charge of the surrounding district, thinking Trimalchio's house was on fire, suddenly burst open the door, and rushing in with water and axes, started the much admired confusion usual under such circumstances. For our part, we seized the excellent opportunity thus offered, snapped our fingers in Agamemnon's face, and away helter-skelter just as if we were escaping from a real conflagration.

CHAPTER ELEVEN

WE had never a torch to guide our wandering steps, while the silent hour of midnight gave small hope of procuring light from chance wayfarers. Added to this was our own intoxication and ignorance of the locality, baffling even by daylight. After dragging our bleeding feet for the best part of an hour over all sorts of stumbling-blocks and fragments of projecting paving-stones, we were finally saved by Giton's ingenuity. For being afraid even by daylight of missing his way, he had taken the precaution the day before to mark every post and pillar on the road with chalk. The strokes he had drawn were visible on the darkest night, their conspicuous whiteness showing wanderers the way. Though truly we were in no less of a fix, even when we did get to our inn. For the old woman had been swilling so long with her customers, you might have set her afire without her knowing anything about it. And we might very likely has passed the night on the doorstep, had not one of Trimalchio's carriers come up, in charge of ten waggons. Accordingly, without stopping to make any more ado, he burst in the door, and let us in by the same road.

Going to my chamber, I went to bed with my dear lad, and burning with amorous ardour as I was after my sumptuous meal, gave myself up heart and soul to all the delights of love.

Oh! what a night was that! how soft
The couch, ye gods! as many a time and oft
Our lips met burning in o'ermastering bliss,
And interchanged our souls in every kiss.
To mortal cares I bid farewell for aye—
So sweet I find it in thine arms to die!

But my self-congratulations were premature. For no sooner had my enfeebled hands relaxed their tipsy hold than Ascyltos, that everlasting contriver of mischief, drew the boy away from me in the dark and carried him off to his own bed; and there rolling about in wanton excess with another man's minion, the latter either not noticing the fraud or pretending not to, he went off to sleep enfolded in an embrace he had no sort of right to, utterly regardless of all human justice. So when I awoke, and feeling the bed over, found it robbed of delight, I declare by all that lovers hold sacred, I had half a mind to run them both through with my sword where they lay, and make their sleep eternal. But presently adopting safer counsels, I thumped Giton awake, and turning a stern countenance on Ascyltos, said severely, "You have broken faith by your dastardly conduct and sinned against our mutual friendship; remove your things as quick as may be, and go seek another place to be the scene of your abominations."

He made no objection to this, but after we had divided our loot with scrupulous exactness, "Come

now," said he, "let's divide the boy." I thought this
were merely a parting jest. But murderously drawing
a sword, "Never," he cried, "shall you enjoy this prey
you gloat over so selfishly. I've been slighted, and I
must have my share, even if I have to cut it off with
this sword." I followed suit on my side, and wrapping
my cloak round my arm, took up a fighting posture.

In wretched trepidation at our unhappy fury the
boy fell at our knees in tears and begged and besought
us not to repeat in a miserable tavern the tragedy of
the two Theban brothers, nor pollute with each other's
blood the sanctity of so noble a friendship. "But if
murder must be done," he declared, "lo! here I lay
bare my throat; here strike, here bury your points.
'Tis I should die, who have violated the sacred bond
of friendship."

At these entreaties we put up our swords. Then
Ascyltos taking the initiative, said, "I will end this
difference. Let the lad himself follow whom he will,
so that he may be perfectly free to choose his friend
and favourite."

For my part, supposing my long, long, intimacy had
bound the boy to me in ties as strong as those of
blood, I felt not the slightest fear, but gladly and
eagerly accepted the proposal to submit the question
to this arbitrament. Yet the instant the words were
out of my mouth, without a moment's hesitation or
one look of uncertainty, he sprang up and declared
Ascyltos to be his choice.

Thunderstruck at this decision, I threw myself just
as I was and unarmed on my bed, and in my despair

would certainly have laid violent hands on myself,
had I not grudged such a victory to my adversary.
Off goes Ascyltos in triumph with his prize, leaving
me forlorn in a strange place—me who so short a while
before had been his dearest comrade and the partner
in all his escapades.

Friendship's a name, expediency's mate,
The shifting symbol of the changing slate.
While Fortune's on our side, our friends stay true;
Let her once change, farewell the recreant crew!
So on the stage, one play's a father's part,
A son's, a rich man's, each with pliant art;
But when the play is ended, grave or gay,
Dropped is the mask, and truth resumes her sway.

However I had no time to indulge my grief, but
dreading lest, to complete my misfortune, Menelaus,
the under-professor, should find me alone at the inn,
I collected my traps together, and with a sad heart
went off to hire a solitary lodging near the sea-shore.
Shutting myself up for three days there, my loneliness
and humiliation for ever haunting my mind, I spent
my time in beating my poor breast, and with many
a deep-drawn groan, crying again and again, "Oh!
why has not the earth swallowed me? why has the
sea, that drowns the guiltless mariner, spared me?
Have I escaped the law, cheated the gallows, slain my
host, that after so many proofs of spirit, I should be
lying here a beggar and a vagabond, alone and forlorn
in the inn of a paltry Greek city? And who is it has
brought me to this desolation? A stripling defiled with

every lust, who on his own admission deserves to be
banished, who won his freedom and enfranchisement
by the prostitution of his body, whose youthful favours
were sold to the highest bidder, who was hired out
as a girl, when known to be a boy all the while. And
what was the other? one who donned on the day of
puberty the woman's frock in lieu of the manly gown,
who was bent from his mother's womb on changing
sex, who was whore to a barrackful of slaves, who
after playing me false and exchanging the instrument
of his lust, abandoned his old friend and, oh! the
infamy of it! like a common strumpet sold everything
in one night's vile work. Now the lovers lie twined
in each other's arms whole nights together, and it may
be, as they rest exhausted after mutual excesses, make
mock of my loneliness. But they shall not go unpunished. As I am a man, and a Roman citizen, I will
avenge the wrong they have done me in their guilty
blood!"

So saying, I gird on a sword, and that bodily weakness might not hinder my warlike intentions, recruit
my strength with a copious meal. Presently I sally
forth, and stalk like a madman through all the public
colonnades. As I was prowling thus, with haggard,
ferocious looks that threatened sheer blood and
slaughter, ever and anon clapping my hand to the hilt
of the weapon I had devoted to my vengeance, a
soldier observed me—if a simple soldier indeed he was,
and not some nocturnal footpad. "Ho, there! comrade," he cried, "what's your legion, and who's your
Centurion?" I named both legion and Centurion with

confident mendacity. "Come, come," he retorted, "do the men of your division go about the streets in Greek pumps?" Then, my face and my agitation sufficiently betraying the imposture, he ordered me to drop my weapon and have a care I did not get into trouble. So despoiled and deprived of my means of vengeance, I retrace my steps to the inn, and my resolution gradually slipping away, I begin to feel nothing but gratitude to the footpad for his bold interference. It never does to trust too much to foresight, for Fortune has her own way of doing things.

Meantime I found it no easy task to overcome my thirst for revenge, and spent half the night in anxious debate. In hopes however, of beguiling my melancholy and forgetting my wrongs, I rose at dawn and visited all the different colonnades, finally entering a Picture Gallery, containing admirable paintings in various styles. There I beheld Zeuxis' handiwork, still unimpaired by the lapse of years, and scanned, not without a certain awe, some sketches of Protogenes', that vied with Nature herself in their truth of presentment. Then I reverently admired the work of Apelles, of the kind the Greeks call "monochromatic"; for such was the exquisite delicacy and precision with which the figures were outlined, you seemed to see the very soul portrayed. Here was the eagle towering to the sky and bearing Ganymede in its talons. There the fair Hylas, struggling in the embraces of the amorous Naiad. Another work showed Apollo cursing his murderous hand, and bedecking his unstrung lyre with blossoms of the new-sprung hyacinth.

Standing surrounded by these painted images of famous lovers, I ejaculated as if in solitary self-communion, "Love, so it seems, troubles even the gods. Jupiter could discover no fitting object of his passion in heaven, his own domain; but though condescending to earthly amours, yet he wronged no trusting heart. Hylas' nymph that ravished him would have checked her ardour, had she known Hercules would come to chide her passion. Apollo renewed the memory of his favourite in a flower; and all these fabled lovers had their way without a rival's interference. But I have taken to my bosom a false-hearted friend more cruel than Lycurgus."

But lo! while I am thus complaining to the winds of heaven, there entered the colonnade an old white-headed man, with a thought-worn face, that seemed to promise something mysterious and out of the common. Yet his dress was far from imposing, making it evident he belonged to the class of men of letters, so ill looked upon by the rich. This man now came up to me, saying, "Sir! I am a poet, and I trust of no mean genius, if these crowns mean anything,—which I admit unfair partiality often confers on unworthy recipients. 'Why then,' you will ask, 'are you so poorly clad?' Just because I am a genius; when did love of art ever make a man wealthy?

The sea-borne trafficker gains pelf untold;
The hardy soldier wins his spoil of gold;
The sycophant on Tyrian purple lies;

The base adulterer with Crœsus vies.
Learning alone, in shuddering rags arrayed,
Vainly invokes th' indifferent Muses' aid!

"No doubt about it; if any man declare himself the
foe of every vice, and start boldly on the path of recti-
tude, in the first place the singularity of his principles
makes him odious—for who can approve habits so
different from his own? Secondly men whose one idea
is to pile up the dollars cannot bear that others should
have a nobler creed than they live by themselves. So
they spite all lovers of literature in every possible way,
to put them into their proper place—below the money-
bags."

"I cannot understand why poverty is always talent's
sister," I said and heaved a sigh.

"You do well," returned the old man, "to deplore the
lot of men of letters."

"Nay!" I replied, "that was not why I sighed; I
have another and a far heavier reason for my sorrow!"
—and immediately, following the common propensity
of mankind to pour one's private griefs into another's
ear, I told him all my misfortunes, inveighing particularly against Ascyltos' perfidy, and ejaculating with
many a groan, "Would to heaven my enemy, the cause
of my present enforced continence, had any vestige
of good feeling left to work upon; but 'tis a hardened
sinner, more cunning and astute than the basest
pander."

Pleased by my frankness, the old man tried to comfort me; and in order to divert my melancholy

thoughts, told me of an amorous adventure that had once happened to himself.

"When I went to Asia," he began, "as a paid officer in the Quaestor's suite, I lodged with a family at Pergamus. I found my quarters very pleasant, first on account of the convenience and elegance of the apartments, and still more so because of the beauty of my host's son. I devised the following method to prevent the master of the house entertaining any suspicions of me as a seducer. Whenever the conversation at table turned on the abuse of handsome boys, I showed such extreme indignation and protested with such an air of austerity and offended dignity against the violence done to my ears by filthy talk of the sort, that I came to be regarded, especially by the mother, as one of the greatest of moralists and philosophers. Before long I was allowed to take the lad to the gymnasium; it was I that directed his studies, I that guided his conduct, and guarded against any possible debaucher of his person being admitted to the house.

"It happened on one occasion that we were sleeping in the dining-hall,—the school having closed early as it was a holiday, and our amusements having rendered us too lazy to retire to our sleeping-chambers. Somewhere about midnight I noticed that the lad was awake; so whispering soft and low, I murmured a timid prayer in these words, 'Lady Venus, if I may kiss this boy, so that he know it not, to-morrow I will present him with a pair of doves.' Hearing the price offered for the gratification, the boy set up a snore. So approaching him, where he lay still making pretence to be asleep, I stole two or three flying kisses. Satisfied with this beginning, I rose betimes next morning, and discharged my vow by bringing the eager lad a choice pair of doves.

"The following night, the same opportunity occurring, I changed my petition, 'If I may pass a naughty hand over this boy, and he not feel it, I will present him for his complaisance with a brace of the best fighting cocks ever seen.' At this promise the child came nestling up to me of his own accord, and was actually afraid, I think, lest I might drop asleep again. I soon quieted his uneasiness on this point, and amply satisfied my longings, short of the supreme bliss, on every part of his beautiful body. Then when daylight came, I made him happy with the gift I had promised him.

"As soon as the third night left me free to try again, I rose as before, and creeping up to the rascal, who was lying awake expecting me, whispered at his ear, 'If only, ye Immortal Gods, I may win of this sleeping darling full and happy satisfaction of my love, for such bliss I will to-morrow present the lad with an Asturian of the Macedonian strain, the best to be had for money, but always on the condition he shall not feel my violence.' Never did the stripling sleep more sound. So first I handled his blump and snowy bosom, then kissed him on the mouth, and finally concentrated all my ardours in one supreme delight. Next morning he sat still in his room, expecting my present as usual. Well! you know as well as I do, it is a much easier matter to buy doves and fighting cocks than an Asturian; besides which, I was afraid so valuable a present might rouse suspicion as to the real motives of my liberality. After walking about for an hour or so, I returned to the house, and gave the boy a kiss—and nothing else. He looked about inquiringly, then threw his arms round my neck, and 'Please, sir!' he said, 'where is my Asturian?'

" 'It is hard,' I replied, 'to get one fine enough. You will have to wait a few days for me to fulfill my vow.'

"The boy had wits enough to see through my answer, and his resentment was betrayed by the angry look that crossed his face.

"Although by this breach of faith I had closed against myself the door of access so carefully contrived, I returned once more to the attack. For, after allowing a few days to elapse, one night when similar circumstances had created just such another opportunity for us as before, I began, the moment I heard the father snoring, to beg and pray the boy to be friends with me again,—that is to let me give him pleasure for pleasure, adding all the arguments my burning concupiscence could suggest. But he was positively angry and refused to say one word beyond, 'Go to sleep, or I will tell my father.' But there is never an obstacle so difficult audacity will not vanquish it. He was still repeating, 'I will wake my father,' when I slipped into his bed and took my pleasure of him in spite of his half-hearted resistance. However he found a certain pleasure in my naughty ways, for after a string of complaints about my having cheated and cajoled him and made him the laughing-stock of his school-fellows, to whom he had boasted of his rich friend, he whispered, 'Still I won't be so unkind as you; if you like, do it again.' So forgetting all our differences, I was reconciled to the dear lad once more, and after utilizing his kind permission, I slipped off to sleep in his arms. But the stripling was not satisfied with only one repetition, all ripe for love as he was and just at the time of life for passive enjoyment. So he woke me up from my slumbers, and, 'Anything you'd like, eh?' said he. Nor was I, so far, indisposed to accept his offer. So working him the best ever I could, to the accompaniment of much panting and perspiration, I gave him what he wanted, and then dropped asleep again, worn out with pleasure. Less than an hour had passed before he started pinching me and asking, 'Eh! why are we not at work?' Hereupon, sick to death of being so often disturbed, I flew into a regular rage, and retorted his own words upon him; 'Go to sleep,' I cried, 'or I'll tell your father!'"

Enlivened by this discourse, I now began to question my companion, who was better informed on these points than myself, as to the dates of the different pictures and the subjects of some that baffled me. At the same time I asked him the reason of the supineness of the present day and the utter decay of the highest branches of art, and amongst the rest of painting, which now showed not the smallest vestige of its former excellence.

"It is greed of money," he replied, "has wrought the change. In early days, when plain worth was still

esteemed, the liberal arts flourished, and the chief
object of men's emulation was to ensure no discovery
likely to benefit future ages long remaining unde-
veloped. To this end Democritus extracted the juices
of every herb, and spent his life in experimenting, that
no virtue of mineral or plant might escape detection.
Similarly Eudoxus grew grey on the summit of a lofty
mountain, observing the motions of the stars and
firmament, while Chrysippus thrice purged his brain
with hellebore, to stimulate its capacity and inventive-
ness. But to consider the sculptors only,—Lysippus
was so absorbed in the modelling of a single figure
that he actually perished from lack of food, and
Myron, who came near embodying the very souls of
men and beasts in bronze, died too poor to find an
heir. But we, engrossed with wine and women, have
not the spirit to appreciate the arts already discovered;
we can only criticize Antiquity, and devote all our
energies, in precept and practice, to the faults of the
old masters. What is become of Dialectic? of As-
tronomy? of Philosophy, that richly cultivated domain? Who nowadays has ever been known to enter
a temple and engage to pay a vow, of only he may
attain unto Eloquence, or find the fountain of wisdom?
Not even do sound intellect and sound health any
longer form the objects of men's prayers, but before
ever they set food on the threshold of the Capitol,
they promise lavish offerings, one if he may bury a
wealthy relative, another if he may unearth a treasure,
another if only he may live to reach his thirty million.
The very Senate, the example of all that is right and

good, is in the habit of promising a thousand pounds
of gold to Capitoline Jove, and that no man may be
ashamed of the lust of pelf, bribes the very God of
Heaven. What wonder then if Painting is in decay,
when all, gods and men alike, find a big lump of gold
a fairer sight than anything those crack-brained Greek
fellows, Apelles and Phidias, ever wrought.

"But there! I see your attention is riveted on that
picture representing the capture of Troy; so I will
endeavour to expound the theme in a copy of verses:

"Still the tenth summer saw the Phrygian host
A prey to doubt and fear, and Calchas' faith
Wavering and weak in spite of oracles,
When at Apollo's word, the wooded heights
Of topmost Ida lent their tallest trees
To shape the frame-work of a monstrous horse.
Within, a vasty cave and secret halls,
Capacious of an army, hold the flower
Of all the Greeks, by ten years' strife enraged;
Their own thank-offering hides th' avenging crew!
Oh! my unhappy country! now we dreamed
A thousand ships were scattered, and our land
Freed from the foe. So ran the lying words
Writ on the horse's flank, and so the tale
Of Sinon's wheedling tongue and traitor's heart.

Now through the gates, glad to be free at last,
The shouting Trojans hail the pledge of peace,
While tears relieve the tension of their joy.
But terror checked their triumph; lo! the priest

Of Neptune, wise Laocoon, his locks unbound,
With cries of warning stays the eager crowd!
His brandished spear he hurled, but foiled by fate,
The blow falls harmless, and the sight renews
Their ill-starred confidence in Grecian guile.
Yet once again he summons all his strength,
And drives his axe deep in the monster's side.
Th' imprisoned warriors' groan resounds, and fills
The wooden hull with terror not its own.
In vain! the captives ride to capture Troy,
And end the tedious war by fraud, not force.

Another marvel! where above the deep
Tower the sheer cliffs of Tenedos, the surge
Is lashed to foam, and a fierce roaring breaks
The silence of the seas, as on a quiet night
The sound of pulsing oars is borne to land,
When fleets are passing on the distant main.
We turn our gaze; and there with rolling coils
Two water-snakes are sweeping towards the shore;
Their flanks, like lofty ships, throw back the foam,
They lash the main, their crests that ride the waves
Gleam fiery like their eyes, whose lightning flash
Kindles the deep, the billows hiss and roar.
All stare aghast. Behold, like priests attired
In Phrygian robes, there stand Laocoon's sons,
Twin pledges of his love, whom in their folds
The fiery snakes entwine. Each lifts his hands,
His childish hands, to guard,—alas! in vain,—
His brother's head; from love's unselfishness
Remorseless death a sharper anguish wins.

Their sire, too weak to save them, shares their fate.
Gorged with fresh blood, the monsters drag him
    down;
Weltering in gore at his own altar's side
The priest a victim dies, in agony
Beating the ground. Thus from polluted shrines
The gods of fated Troy were driven away.

The rising Moon her beam had just displayed,
Kindling her radiant torch amid the stars,
When the impatient Greeks unbar the doors;
And forth on Troy, by sleep and wine betrayed,
The steel-clad warriors rush, as from the yoke
Just loosed, a gallant steed of Thessaly
Darts o'er the course tossing his eager mane.
They draw their flashing blades and wave their
    shields
And 'havoc!' cries. One stabs the sleeping sot
With wine oppressed, one from the altar flames
Snatches a burning brand and fires the town,—
And Troy's own temples arm her foemen's hands."

Sundry of the public who were strolling in the
Colonnades now proceeded to pelt the reciter with
stones. But Eumolpus, who was familiar with the sort
of applause his talents usually met with, merely covered
up his head and bolted from the Temple, I was afraid
he would claim me as a poet. So I started off in pursuit
of the fugitive, and came up with him on the seashore.
There we halted, directly we were out of range of
the missiles, and I asked him, "Now what do you

mean by this confounded malady of yours? I have not been a couple of hours in your company, and you've talked oftener like a mad poet than a sensible man. I don't wonder the populace pelts you. I am going to fill my pocket with stones, and every time I see your wits going, I shall bleed you in the head."

At this he changed countenance, and "Oh! my young friend," he said, "to-day is by no means my first essay; every time I've entered a theatre to recite some trifle, the audience invariably welcomes me with this kind of treat. However as I am far from wishing to quarrel with you, I undertake to keep a whole day's fast from poetry."

"Very well then," said I, "if you'll abjure your crankiness for to-day, we'll dine together." So saying, I commissioned the housekeeper at my humble rooms to make preparations for our humble meal, and we went off straight to the baths.

CHAPTER TWELVE

Arrived at the baths, I catch sight of Giton laden
with towels and scrapers, leaning against a wall and
wearing a look of melancholy embarrassment on his
face. You could easily see he was an unwilling servant; and indeed, to show my eyes had not deceived
me, he now turned upon me a countenance beaming
with pleasure, saying, "Oh! have pity on me, brother!
there are no weapons to fear here, so I can speak
freely. Save me, save me, from the murderous ruffian;
and then lay upon your judge, now your penitent, any
punishment you please, no matter how severe. It
will be comfort enough for me in my misery to have
perished by your good pleasure."

I bade him hush his complaints, that no one might
surprise our plans, and leaving Eumolpus to his own
devices,—he was engaged in reciting a poem to his fellow bathers,—ı dragged Giton down a dark and dirty
passage, and so hurried him away to my lodging.
Then after bolting the door, I threw my arms round his
neck, pressing my lips convulsively to his tear-stained
face. It was long before either of us could find his
voice; for my darling's bosom was quivering like my
own with quick-coming sobs. "I am ashamed of my
criminal weakness," I cried, "but I love you still,
though you did forsake me, and the wound that

pierced my heart has left not a scar behind. What can you say to excuse your surrender to another? Did I deserve so base a wrong?"

Seeing he was still loved, he put on a less downcast look:

To chide, to love,—how make these two agree?
The task beyond e'en Hercules would be.
Let Love appear, all angry passions cease.

"Yet," I could not help adding, "I never meant to refer the choice of whom you should love to any third person; but there! all is forgiven and forgotten, if only you show yourself sincerely penitent." My words were interspersed with groans and tears; when I had done, the dear boy dried my cheeks with his mantle, saying, "I beg you, Encolpius, let me appeal to your own recollection of the circumstances. Did I desert you, or did you throw me over? I am ready to confess,—and it is my best excuse,—when I saw you both sword in hand, I fled for safety to the stronger fighter." Kissing the bosom so full of wise prudence, I threw my arms round his neck, and to let him see he was restored to favour and my affection and confidence were as strong as ever, I pressed him closely to my heart.

It was quite dark and the woman had completed my orders for dinner when Eumolpus knocked at the door. I called out, "How many of you are there?" and immediately proceeded to spy through a chink in the door to see whether Ascyltos had not come too. But seeing my guest was alone, I at once hastened to let him in. He threw himself on my pallet, and directly he observed Giton moving about in attendance he wagged his head and remarked, "I like your Ganymede; we shall have a good time to-day." I was anything but pleased with this indiscreet beginning, and began to fear I had opened my doors to another Ascyltos. Eumolpus grew more and more pressing, and on the lad's serving him with wine, "I like you better," he said, "than any of them at the Baths;" and draining his cup thirstily, added he had never been more vexed in his life. "I tell you, at the Bath just now, I came very near getting a beating, merely because I tried to repeat a copy of verses to the bathers sitting around the basin. It was just like the Theatre—I was turned out of the place. Then I started to look for you in every corner of the building, shouting Encolpius! Encolpius! at the top of my voice. Not far off a naked youth, who had lost his clothes, and roaring with just the same clamorous indignation after Giton. For me, I was treated like a madman by the very slave lads, who mocked and mimicked me most insolently; he on the contrary was soon surrounded by a thronging multitude, clapping their hands and showing the most awe-struck admiration. The fact is, he possessed virile parts of such enormous mass and weight, the man really seemed only an appendage of his own member. Oh; an indefatigable worker! I warrant, the sort to begin yesterday, and finish tomorrow! Accordingly he soon found a way out of his difficulties; a bystander, a Roman knight, they said, of notorious character, wrapped his own cloak round the poor wanderer, and took him home with him, in order I imagine to have the sole enjoyment of so rich a windfall. But I should never have recovered so much as my own clothes from the Bathkeeper, had I not produced some one to vouch for me. So much better does it profit a man to train his member than his mind?"

During Eumolpus's narrative I changed countenance repeatedly, now jubilant at my hated rival's misfortunes, now saddened by his success. I held my tongue, however, pretending to know nothing of the matter, and set to work arranging the dinner table. I had hardly finished this, when our humble repast was brought in; the fare was homely, but succulent and substantial, and Eumolpus, our famished scholar, fell to with a will, extolling the simplicity of the viands in the following lines:

All things that may our simple wants assuage
Kind heaven bestows to ease our hunger's rage;
Wild herbs and berries from the woodland spray
Suffice the craving appetite to stay.
What man would thirst beside a stream, or stand
To front the wintry blast with fire at hand?
The law is armed to guard the marriage bed,
The chaste bride blameless yields her maidenhead.
Whate'er is needful, bounteous Nature gives;
Pride only in unbridled riot lives!

After satisfying his appetite, our philosopher began to moralize, indulging in many criticisms of such as despise familiar things and attach value only to what

is rich and rare. To their perverted taste anything
that is allowable is held cheap, while they display a
morbid predilection for forbidden luxuries.

Facile success, a rose without a thorn,
An instant victory, are things I scorn.
The Phasian bird from distant Colchis brought
And Afric fowl! are dainties ever sought,
For these are rarities; not so the goose
And bright-plumed duck, fit but for vulgar use.

The costly scar, choice fish from Syrtes' shore,
That cost poor fishers' lives, these all adore;
The mullet's out of date. The modern man
Deserts his wife to woo the courtesan;
The rose yields place to cinnamon. For naught
Is held of worth that is not dearly bought.

"Is this the way," I cried, "you keep your promise
of making no more poetry to-day? On your con-
science, spare us at least, who have never thrown a
stone at you. Once let any one of the company drinking under the same roof with us scent out your poet-
ship, he will rouse the whole neighbourhood and overwhelm us all in the same ruin. Have some pity on
your friends, and remember the picture gallery and
the baths." But Giton, who was all gentleness, re-
monstrated with me for speaking so, and declared I
was doing ill thus to jeer at my elders. He said I
was forgetting my duty as a host, and after inviting
a man to my table out of compassion, was nullifying

the obligation by then insulting him. Other remarks
follow, all equally imbued with moderation and good
sense, and coming with added grace from so beautiful
a mouth.

"Happy the mother of such a son!" exclaimed
Eumolpus. "Go on, good youth, and prosper! Rare
indeed is such a combination of wisdom and beauty.
Never think all your words have been wasted; you
have won a lover! I, I will extol your praises in my
verse. I will be your preceptor and your guardian,
your companion everywhere, even when unbidden.
Nor has Encolpius anything to complain of, who loves
another." The speaker had much to thank the soldier
for who had taken my sword from me; otherwise the
wrath I had conceived against Ascyltos would surely
have been wreaked on Eumolpus's head. Giton saw
what was toward, and slipped out of the room, as if
to fetch water; and his judicious departure abated the
extreme heat of my indignation. My anger cooled a
little, and I told Eumolpus, "Sir! I would rather have
you talking poetry than entertaining such hopes as
these. I am a passionate man, and you a lecherous;
our characters, look you, can never accord together.
Suppose me stark mad: humour my frenzy,—in other
words, leave the house without a moment's delay."

Confounded at this outburst, Eumolpus never
stopped to ask my reasons, but instantly left the room,
drew the door to after him, and locked me in, to my
intense surprise. He carried off the key with him, and
hurried away at a run in search of Giton.

Finding myself a prisoner, I resolved to hang my-

self and so end my miseries. I had already attached
my girdle to the framework of a bed which stood
against the wall, and was just fitting the noose round
my neck, when the doors were flung open again, and
Eumolpus coming in with Giton recalled me to the
light of life from the fatal bourne I had so nearly
passed. Giton especially, his agony turning to rage and
fury, uttered a piercing shriek, and pushing me down
headlong on the bed with both hands, "You deceive
yourself, Encolpius," he cried, "if you think you can
contrive to die before me. I was first; I have already
been to Ascyltos's lodging to look for a sword. Had
I not found you, I was going to hurl myself over a
precipice. Now, to show you Death is never far from
those who seek him, behold in your turn the sight you
intended me to witness."

With these words he snatches a razor from Eumolpus's hired servant, and drawing it once and again
across his throat, tumbles down at our feet. Uttering
a cry of horror, I fall on the floor beside him, and
seek to take my own life with the same weapon. But
neither did Giton exhibit the smallest sign of a wound,
nor did I myself feel any pain. The fact is, the razor
had no edge, coming from a case of razors purposely
blunted, with the object of training barbers' ap-
prentices to a proper confidence in the exercise of their
craft; and that was why the servant from whom he
snatched the instrument had expressed no sort of consternation, nor had Eumolpus made an effort to hinder
the mimic tragedy.

In the midst of this lovers' fooling, the landlord

enters with another course of the dinner, and staring hard at us where we lay sprawling disgracefully on the floor, "Are you all drunk," he asked, "or runaways,—or both? Now who put up that bed against the wall like that? and what do all these underhanded proceedings mean? By great Hercules, you intended, you scamps, to levant in the night, and get out of paying the rent for your room. Not so fast, I say. I'll let you know it's no poor widow woman's the owner of the block, but Marcus Mannicius." "You threaten, do you?" shouts Eumolpus, and fetches the man a good sharp slap in the face. The latter hurled at his head an earthenware jar, emptied by a succession of thirsty guests, cut open his noisy adversary's forehead, and darted out of the room. Furious at the indignity, Eumolpus snatches up a wooden candlestick, pursues the fugitive, and revenges his injury with a shower of blows. The whole household comes crowding to the scene of action, together with a mob of drunken customers. Now was my opportunity for retaliation; so I turn the tables on Eumolpus by shutting the blackguard out, and find myself without a rival and free to do as I please with my room and my night.

Meanwhile the unfortunate Eumolpus, being locked out, is assaulted by the scullions and miscellaneous tenants of the block. One threatens his eyes with a spit loaded with hissing-hot guts; another snatches a flesh-hook from the kitchen hearth and assumes a fighting attitude. First and foremost, an old hag with sore eyes and a most filthy apron, and mounted on wooden clogs (an odd pair) hauls in a huge dog on a chain, and sets him at Eumolpus, who however made a gallant defence against all assailants with his candlestick. All this we saw through a hole in the door, just made by the wrenching off of the handle of the wicket, and for my own part I wished him joy of his beating. Giton on the contrary, with his usual tender-heartedness, was for opening the door and rescuing him from his perilous position. My resentment being still hot within me, I could not hold my hand, but favoured the poet's sympathizer with a good smart box on the side of the head, at which he went and sat down crying on the bed. For myself, I put first one eye, then the other, to the opening, and was regaling myself with the sight of Eumolpus's sorry plight and mentally patting his assailants on the back, when Bargates, the agent of the block, who had been called away from his dinner, was borne into the heart of the skirmish by a couple of chairmen, for he was disabled by the gout. After a long harangue against drunkards and runaways, uttered in a savage tone and barbarous accent, he said, turning upon Eumolpus, "My prince of poets, you here? and these ruffianly slaves don't fly at once and stop their brawling!" Then putting his lips to Eumolpus's ear, "My bedfellow," he went on, in a more subdued tone, "is a scornful jade; so if you love me, blackguard her in verse, will you, to make her feel ashamed of herself."

Whilst Eumolpus was talking apart with Bargates, a crier attended by a public slave and a small crowd of curious persons besides, entered the inn, and brandishing a torch that gave more smoke than light, read out the following public notice:

"Lost or strayed lately in the Baths, a boy,—aged sixteen, curly-headed, a minion by trade, good-looking, Giton by name. Whoever will bring back the same or give information of his present whereabouts, will receive a thousand sesterces reward."

Not far from the herald stood Ascyltos in a particoloured robe, exhibiting description, and voucher for the sum promised, on a silver platter. I told Giton to dash under the bed and twist his hands and feet into the cords by which the mattress was supported on the framework, so that stretched full length underneath, like Ulysses of old clinging under the ram's belly, he might escape any prying hands. Giton promptly obeyed, and in another instant had cleverly twisted his fingers in the attachments, and beaten the wily Ulysses at his own game. For my part, so as to leave no room for suspicion, I heaped the pallet with clothes, and shaped an impression amongst them of a single sleeper, and that a man of my own size.

Meantime Ascyltos, visiting each room in succession with the apparitor, arrived at mine, where his hopes of success rose the higher on finding the door so carefully barred. But the public slave, inserting his axe in the crack of the door, broke the hold of the fastenings. Thereupon I threw myself at Ascyltos' feet and implored him by the memory of our former friendship and our companionship in misfortune at any rate to let me see Giton. Nay! more, to give colour to my pretended supplication, "I am well aware, Ascyltos," I cried, "that you have come to murder me; why else have you brought these axes with you? Take your revenge then; see, I offer my neck, so shed my life's blood, which you are seeking under pretence of searching my room."

Ascyltos protested indignantly against the imputation, asseverating he was there only to look for his runaway favourite; he desired, he said, no man's, certainly no suppliant's death, and least of all that of a man whom, even after our fatal quarrel, he still thought of as his dearest friend.

Nor was the public slave idle meanwhile, but snatching a cane from the innkeeper, he thrusts it under the bed, and even investigates every cranny in the walls. Giton kept shirking away from the stick, and holding his breath in abject terror, squeezed closer and closer, till the bugs were tickling his very nose.

Scarcely had the men left the room when Eumolpus, for the shattered door could keep no one out, dashes in in great excitement, shouting, "The thousand sesterces are mine; I shall now run after the officer and denounce you, as you richly deserve, and inform him Giton is in your hands at the present moment." I embrace the poet's knees, but he remains obdurate; I beseech him not to kill the dying; I tell him, "Your resolution would have some sense in it, if you could produce the missing boy, but he has disappeared in the crowd, and I cannot so much as guess where he is gone to. In heaven's name, Eumolpus, bring the lad back and restore him to his friends,—to Ascyltos, if it must be so."

He was just beginning to credit my plausible story when Giton, all but smothered and choking for breath, give three loud sneezes one after the other, so that the bed positively shook. Eumolpus wheeled round at the commotion, exclaiming, "Giton, God bless you!" Then lifting the mattress away, he reveals Ulysses in such a plight even a half-starving Cyclops might well have spared him! Next turning to me, "What is the meaning of all this, you thief?" said he. "What! even when found out, you had not spirit enough to tell the truth. In fact, if some God that governs human affairs had not made the boy betray where he hung concealed, I should have been sent wandering from tavern to tavern on a wild goose chase."

Giton, a far better wheedler than myself, first staunched the wound in the poor man's forehead with some cobwebs dipped in oil; then exchanged his own little cloak for the other's torn robe, and seeing him somewhat mollified, kissed his bruises to make them well, crying, "We are in your keeping, in your hands, dearest father! If you love your Giton, try, oh! try to save him. I would the consuming fire might scorch me to ashes, the raging waters overwhelm me, and me alone! For 'tis I am the subject, I the cause, of all these wicked doings! My death would reconcile two enemies."

Touched by our troubles, and above all stirred by Giton's blandishments, Eumolpus exclaimed, "Fools, fools; gifted as you are with qualities to ensure your happiness, you persist in leading a life of wretchedness, and every day by your own acts draw down fresh torments on your heads. My plan of life has always been, so to spend each day as if it were my last, that is in peace and quietness; if you would follow my example, dismiss all anxious thoughts from your minds. Ascyltos persecutes you here; then fly his neighbourhood, and come with me on a voyage I am about to make to foreign parts. I sail as a passenger in a vessel that may very likely weigh this very night; I am well known on board, and we shall be sure of a hearty welcome."

Take ship, brave youth, and seek in other lands
Where brighter fortunes wait on willing hands.
Keep a bold heart; let furthest Ister know
Thy mettle, and old Nile, and ice and snow
Of Arctic seas. Range East, range West, in thee
Let new found climes a new Ulysses see!

His advice appeared to me sound and good, as it was likely to free me from further annoyance on the part of Ascyltos, and at the same time gave promise of a happier existence. Overwhelmed by Eumolpus's generosity, I felt profoundly sorry for the insults I had just been offering him and very penitent for my jealousy, which had given rise to so many calamities. With floods of tears I begged and prayed him to include me too in his forgiveness, pointing out that it was beyond the power of lovers to control the frenzies of jealousy. I pledged myself for the future to do or say nothing whatever that could give him offence, and urged him to banish all irritation from his mind, as a learned and educated man should, so that not a trace of injury should remain. "On rugged and un-cultivated ground," I went on, "the snow lies long, but where the soil has been disciplined and improved by the plough, the light snowfall melts away before you can say it has fallen. It is the same with resentment in men's hearts; it abides long in uncultured minds, but melts quickly from the surface of such as have been trained and educated." "To prove the truth of what you say," returned Eumolpus, "I hereby end my anger with this kiss. So in luck's name, pack up your traps and follow me, or if you so prefer, lead the way yourselves."

The words were still on his lips when the door flew open with a crash, and a rough-bearded sailor appeared on the threshold, who shouted, "You're all behind, Eumolpus; don't you know the Blue Peter's flying?"

In an instant we were all afoot. Eumolpus wakes his servant who had long ago dropped asleep, and orders him off with his baggage. Giton and I pack up all our belongings for the journey, and after a prayer to the stars, make our way on board.

CHAPTER THIRTEEN

WE chose out a retired spot on the stern-deck, and as it was not even yet daylight, Eumolpus dozed off; but neither Giton nor myself could get a single wink of sleep. I reflected with anxiety on the fact that I had made a companion of Eumolpus, a still more redoubtable rival than Ascyltos, and the thought gave me no peace. But reason presently getting the better of my chagrin, "It is certainly unfortunate," I said to myself, "that our friend finds the boy so much to his liking; but then are not all Nature's finest productions common to all mankind? The sun shines on the just and on the unjust. The moon, with her countless train of attendant stars, lights the very beasts of the wilderness to their prey. What can be more beautiful than water? Yet it flows freely for all and sundry. Is Love alone to be furtively snatched and not won in the open field? Nay! for my own part, I would rather not have any good thing that all the world may not covet. One rival, and that an old man, will hardly do me much harm; even should he wish to presume, he will but lose his labour, for want of breath." Reassured by the unlikelihood of his success, I calmed my anxieties, and wrapping my head in my cloak, tried to persuade myself I was asleep. But all of a sudden, as if Fortune were resolved to destroy my composure, a lamentable voice sounded on the poop-deck, crying, "What! has he fooled me then?" It was a man's voice, and one not unfamiliar to my ears, and my heart began to beat wildly. Nor was this all; for now a woman, equally indignant, blazed out in an even fiercer tone, "If only some god would put Giton in my power, what a welcome I would give the vagabond!" Stunned by the unexpectedness of the words, we both turned pale as death. I was particularly terrified, and felt as if I were being tortured by a horrible nightmare. When I found my voice at last, I asked Eumolpus, who was just dropping off to sleep, plucking at the skirt of his tunic with trembling hands, "By all you deem holy, father, whose ship is this? and who are aboard her? tell me that."

He was furious at being disturbed. "So this was the reason," he grumbled, "you chose out the quietest nook on the deck for us to occupy, that you might not allow us one moment's rest? What the better are you, when I've told you Lichas a Tarentine commands the ship, and that Tryphaena is his passenger to Tarentum?" I shuddered horror-struck at this thunderclap, and baring my throat, "Oh! Destiny," I ejaculated, "now truly is your triumph complete!" Giton for his part fell in a dead faint on my bosom. Presently, when a copious sweat had relieved the tension of our spirits, I grasped Eumolpus round the knees, and cried, "Have pity on two dying wretches, and in the name of what we both hold dear, end our life; death draws nigh, and unless you refuse to deal it, will haply be a boon."

Overwhelmed by my odious suspicion, Eumolpus swore by gods and goddesses he knew nothing whatever of what had happened; and had never entertained a thought of treachery; but that in absolute innocence of heart and simple good faith he had led his comrades aboard the ship he had long ago chosen for his own conveyance over-seas. "Come now, what plot is there afoot?" he demanded; "what Hannibal have we on board with us? Lichas of Tarentum, a most respectable man, and not merely owner of this vessel, which he commands himself, but of sundry landed estates besides and a house of commerce, is carrying a cargo to sell in the way of business. So this is the Cyclops, the pirate king, we owe our passage-money to; then besides him, there is Tryphaena, the fairest of fair women, who is sailing from port to port on pleasure bent."

"Why, these," retorted Giton, "are very persons we wish to avoid," and gave the astonished Eumolpus a short account of the reasons for their hostility and the extremity of the risk we ran. So confounded was he at the news, he knew not what advice to offer, but besought each of us to say what he thought. "Imagine us entrapped," he went on, "in the Cyclops' cave; some means or other of escape must be discovered, unless we prefer a leap overboard and a sudden end to all our troubles." "Better," interposed Giton, "persuade the pilot to steer the ship into some harbour, of course making it worth his while, and tell him your brother is so subject to sea-sickness he is at death's door. You can easily colour this excuse with woe-begone

looks and streaming tears, so that the officer may grant
you the favour out of sheer compassion." But
Eumolpus at once declared this scheme to be imprac-
ticable; "for big ships," he pointed out, "require to
be laboriously warped into landlocked harbours; besides how utterly improbable it will sound that the
boy should have come to such a desperate pass so
quickly as all this. Another point,—most likely Lichas
will want to visit a sick passenger as a mark of civility.
How singularly pleasant for us, look you, to have the
captain, whom we particularly wish to avoid, coming
to see us of his own motion! But again, granted the
vessel could be turned from her main course, and
that Lichas should never think of inspecting the sick
boy, how are we to get off the ship without every soul
on board seeing us? With faces muffled, or faces bare?
If muffled, who but will spring forward to help the
poor patients ashore? If bare, what does this amount
to but simply giving ourselves away?"

"Nay! why not," I interposed, "make a bold stroke,
slip down a rope into the ship's boat and cutting the
painter leave the rest to Fortune? Not that I expect
Eumolpus to join in the venture; why should we in-
volve an innocent man in troubles that in no way concern him? Enough for me if good luck attend us two
on our descent into the boat." "Not at all a bad idea,"
said Eumolpus, "if only it were feasible; but who
could help noticing your attempt,—first and foremost
the pilot, who is on watch all night, observing every
motion of the stars? Possibly you might elude his
vigilance during an instant's sleepiness, if escape were

practicable by any other part of the vessel; but as
things are, you are bound to escape by the stern, past
the very helm, for that is where the rope is made
fast that secures the boat. Besides, I wonder this
never occurred to you, Encolpius, that one of the
crew is on watch in the boat night and day, a sentinel
you cannot get rid of, except by killing the man or
pitching him neck and crop overboard. As to the
feasibility of this, well! consult your own courage.
About my accompanying you myself, I shirk no danger
that gives the faintest hope of success. But to throw
away one's life as a thing of no importance is, I am
sure, what you do not approve of.

"Now consider how you like this plan; I will clap
you in a couple of hides, cording you up among my
clothes as part of my luggage, of course leaving suf-
ficient openings for you to breathe and eat through.
Then I will raise an outcry to the effect that my slaves
have both jumped overboard, because they were afraid
of a more terrible punishment. So when we get into
port, I will convey you ashore as baggage without exciting any suspicion whatever."

"Oh! you would pack us up in bales, as if we were
solid inside, eh?—and not liable to evacuations at all?
as if we never sneezed or snored? The same sort of
trick turned out such a success once before, didn't it?
Granted we could endure the bondage for a day, what
if a calm or a contrary gale prolonged the time further?
what would become of us then? Why! even clothes,
if kept too long tightly packed, cut at the folds, and
papers grow illegible, when tied up in bundles. Young

and unused to hardship, how shall we endure swathing bands and ligaments, like graven images? We must find some better way of escape than this. Listen to what I have hit on. Eumolpus, as a man of letters, of course carries ink about him; let us black ourselves with it from head to foot. Then as Ethiopian slaves we shall be at your service, light-hearted and free from fear of consequences, besting our enemies by this change of complexion."

"Why certainly," cried Giton, "circumcise us too, that we may pass for Jews, and bore our ears to imitate Arabs, and chalk our faces that Gaul may claim us as her sons! As if a change of colour could modify the whole appearance; why! a host of alterations must be united to make the illusion convincing. Grant our dyed faces would keep their black; suppose no touch of water to make the colour run, no blot of ink to stick to our clothes, an accident that will often happen even when no mucilage is added; pray, can we give ourselves the hideous swollen lips of the African? can we transform our hair to wool with curling-tongs? can we scar our brows with rows of ugly wrinkles? render ourselves bow-legged and flat-footed? give our beards that outlandish look? A dye may disfigure the person, it cannot change it. Now hear a desperate man's remedy; let us wind our clothes around our heads, and plunge into the deep."

"Gods and men forbid," cried Eumolpus, "you should end your days in so base a fashion. Better, far better, do as I advise. My servant, as the razor incident showed you, is a barber; let him instantly shave you both,—not heads only but eyebrows as well. I will second his efforts, marking your foreheads with writing, so cleverly executed you will have all the look of a pair of branded slaves. My lettering will at one and the same time divert the suspicions of your pursuers, and under the guise of a degrading punishment, conceal your real features."

This plan was approved, and our metamorphosis effected without delay. We stole to the side of the ship, and submitted our heads and eyebrows too to the barber's tender mercies. Eumolpus then proceeded to cover both our foreheads with enormous capital letters, and with a liberal hand sprawl the well known sign of runaways all over our faces. It so happened that one of the passengers, who was leaning over the side unburdening his sea-sick stomach, privately noted the barber busied with this unseasonable moonlight work, and with a curse at the sinister omen of an act so nearly resembling the last despairing vow of ship-wrecked mariners, hurried back to his berth. Feigning indifference to the sufferer's imprecation, we fell into the same melancholy train of thought as before, and settling down in silence, spent the remaining hours of darkness in an uneasy doze.

Next day, directly Eumolpus learned Tryphaena was arisen, he entered Lichas's cabin; here after some conversation about the prosperous voyage promised by the fine weather, Lichas remarked, turning to Tryphaena, "Priapus appeared to me in a dream last night, and said, 'Encolpius, the man you are in search of, I hereby tell you, has by me been brought on board your ship.'" Tryphaena started violently; "You might think we had slept together," she exclaimed; "for I too saw a vision, that image of Nepture I noticed in the Temple Court at Baiae, telling me, 'You will find Giton on Lichas's ship.'"

"This will show you plainly," interrupted Eumolpus, "that Epicurus was a man inspired, who most elegantly expresses his opinion of these figments of the imagination:

"Dreams that delude our minds with shadows vain
  Are not heaven-sent. But each man's proper brain
  Forges these nothings; and the mind at play
  Doth nightly re-enact the deeds of day,
  While the tired body sleeps. The conqueror
  Who cities shakes, loosing the dogs of War,
  Sees brandished spears, and routs, and deaths of
    Kings,
  And blood, and all the horrors battle brings.
  What sees the lawyer?—ranged a dreadful show,
  The bench, the bar, the judges all a-row!
  The miser dreams of gold, lost treasure finds.
  Through woodland ways his horn the huntsman
    winds.
  The sailor's vision scenes of wreck describes.
  The harlot wheedles; the adultress bribes.
  The sleeping hound the flying hare pursues;
  And each unhappy wretch old griefs renews."

Lichas, however, after duly expiating Tryphaena's dream, said, "Who is to hinder us searching the ship anyway, that we may not appear to scorn the revelation the gods vouchsafe?"

The passenger who had so unfortunately surprised our furtive manoeuvres during the night, Hesus he was called, now suddenly broke in with the question, "Who were the fellows then that were shaved by moonlight last night,—an abominable thing to do, upon my word! For they tell me it's wicked for any man alive, when aboard ship, to cut either nails or hair, except when the wind is at odds with the waves."

Lichas flew into a passion of anger and consternation at the words, blustering, "Has anyone dared to cut his hair on my ship, and at dead of night too? Produce the culprits instantly, that I may know whose heads must fall to purify my vessel from the taint."

"It was I," Eumolpus confessed, "ordered it. If I have brought down ill luck, I shall not escape my share, for am I not to travel in the same ship? But the fact is the offenders had such monstrously long and shaggy hair I ordered the wretches' unkempt locks to be shorn, that I might not seem to be turning our good ship into a gaol, as also that the letters branded on their brows might be legible to all men's eyes, being no longer overshadowed and hidden by the hair. Amongst other knavish tricks, they have been spending my money on a light-o'-love they kept between them, from whose side I dragged them away only last night reeking with wine and perfumes. Indeed they stink at this minute of the relics of their debauch—at my expense!"

Accordingly, by way of expiation to the tutelary spirit of the ship, it was decreed we should each of us

receive forty stripes. Without further delay the savage
sailors fall upon us, anxious to appease the deity with
our wretched blood. For myself, I digested three
lashes with Spartan fortitude; but Giton, at the very
first blow, set up such a yell his well remembered
voice penetrated straight to Tryphaena's ears. Nor
was the mistress the only one startled by his cries; all
her maids as well, attracted by the familiar tones,
gather round the triangles. Already had his wondrous beauty begun to disarm the sailors and deprecate
their rage with its mute appeal, when Tryphaena's
women all chime in with the cry, "Giton! it's Giton!
stay, oh! stay your savage hands. Help, help, mistress! it's Giton!" Tryphaena turns only too ready an
ear to their words, and flies headlong to his side.
Lichas, who knew me perfectly, just as well as if he
had heard my voice too, now runs up, and looking
neither at hands nor face, but instantly lowering his
eyes to my middle, politely laid his hands on those
parts, and greeted me by my name. Why wonder any
longer at Ulysses' nurse, after twenty years, identifying
the scar that proved his birth, when this most observing master mariner, spite of every lineament of fate
and form being disguised, yet pounced shrewdly on the
sole and only attribute that betrayed the fugitive.
Tryphaena burst into tears, supposing our disfigure-
ment real and that we had been branded on the brow
as slaves, and inquired in soft tones of pity, what
dungeon we had fallen into on our wanderings, or
whose hands had been barbarous enough to inflict so
terrible a punishment. Doubtless they had merited

some mark of ignominy, the runaways, whom her favours had only turned into enemies—but not such a one as this!

Frenzied with indignation, Lichas sprang forward, crying, "Oh! the simplicity of the woman! to actually believe these scars were made and the letters really imprinted, with the branding-iron! I only wish the marks they have disfigured their faces with were permanent! This would be some satisfaction to us at any rate. As a matter of fact, the whole thing's a farce, and the lettering a delusion and a snare!"

Tryphaena was by way of showing some compassion, inasmuch as all was not lost for her pleasures; but Lichas, remembering his wife's seduction and the insults he had received in the portico of the Temple of Hercules, and showing a countenance fiercely contorted with passion, cries, "This will show you, I imagine, Tryphaena, the immortal gods do govern human lives. Have they not brought the culprits all unwitting on board our ship; yea! and warned us of the fact by dreams coinciding in every particular with the truth? Look you now, how can we pardon offenders whom God himself puts into our hands for chastisement? For my part, I'm not a cruel man; but I dare not spare them, lest I suffer for it myself."

Impressed by these superstitious arguments, Tryphaena changed her mind, and declared she would make no further objection to our punishment, but would gladly second so just a piece of retribution. She had received, she added, as cruel wrong as Lichas himself; for had not her good name been publicly traduced before a vulgar mob?

'Twas terror first gave origin to gods,
When the forked lightning, flashing from the sky,
Would o'erwhelm towns and lofty Athos fire.
Next, rising Sun, and waxing, waning Moon,
Offerings received. So idols filled the world,
And not a month but had its proper god.
Far spread the taint; blind superstition led
The rustic swain to pay his first-fruits' toll
To Ceres, and with grapes Bacchus to crown,
And Pales venerate, the shepherd's god;
So Nepture ruled the waves, Pallas the schools.
Each man of mark, each founder of a State,
New gods invents, his rival to outstrip.

Lichas seeing Tryphaena eager as himself for revenge, ordered our punishment to be renewed and increased. On hearing this Eumolpus endeavoured to mitigate his anger by the following speech: "The unhappy beings whose destruction your vengeance claims, imploring your compassion, Lichas; they have chosen me, as one not unknown to you, to the office of mediator, to reconcile them once more to those they formerly held so dear. You cannot really suppose the young men fell into this trap by mere chance; for surely the very first thing an intending passenger asks, is the name of the person he is to intrust his safety to. Relent then; be satisfied with the penalties already exacted, and suffer free men to proceed to their destination without further injury. The harshest and most unforgiving of masters stay their cruelty, when slaves return home penitent; and do we not all of us spare enemies who surrender? What more do you want or desire? Prostrate before you lie these youths, men of birth and breeding though they be, and what is more than this, friends once bound to you in the ties of closest intimacy. Had they embezzled your money, had they betrayed your trust, by great Hercules! even then your resentment might be satisfied with the pains and penalties you behold. Lo! the marks of servitude upon their brows, and their faces—free men's faces—wearing voluntarily the degrading badge of punishment!"

But Lichas cut short the plea of mercy. "Nay! you confuse the issue," he interrupted; "you should keep each point separate and distinct. First of all, if they came here of their own free will, why did they shave their heads? The man who adopts a disguise is after no good, but is trying to deceive. Secondly, if they were seeking forgiveness and reconciliation through your good offices, why did you take every possible pains to keep your clients concealed? It is plain enough the culprits did fall into the trap accidentally, and that you are merely trying on an artful subterfuge to slip out of reach of our resentment.

"Then for your special pleading, your noisy claim about their being men of birth and breeding, have a care you don't injure your case by over-confidence. Whatever is the injured party to do, when the guilty run blindly to their own punishment? But, you urge, they were our friends; the more thoroughly, I say, have they earned their chastisement. The man who wrongs mere strangers, is called a robber; he who betrays his friends, is little better than a murderer."

Eumolpus, to rebut this damaging reasoning, replies, "There is nothing, I gather, tells more heavily against the unfortunate young men than the fact of their having cut off their hair by night; this is taken to prove they did not come on board voluntarily, but by mischance. I only trust my explanation may seem as simple and straightforward as the act itself was simply and innocently done. They purposed, before ever they embarked, to have eased their heads of an annoying and needless burden, but the wind springing up sooner than was expected forced them to put off their visit to the barber; nor did they for an instant imagine it mattered where they carried out the intention they had formed, knowing nothing of the omen involved or the rules aboard ship."

"What made them take the guise of suppliants and shave their heads," was Lichas's only answer—"unless possibly because bald heads are more likely to win compassion? But there, what use trying to get at the truth through an interpreter? What have you to say for yourself, you thief? What salamander has burnt off your eyebrows? what god have you vowed your locks to? Answer me, villain." As for me, I stood dumbfounded, silenced by my terror of punishment, unable in my confusion to find a word, so plain was the case against me. Besides, I was so disfigured, what with my cropped head and my eyebrows as bare as my forehead, I could do nothing and say nothing

becomingly. But when presently my tearful face was
wiped with a wet sponge, and the ink being thus moist-
ened and smeared all over my countenance, my features were all confounded together in one sooty cloud,
his anger turned into disgust. Eumolpus stoutly declared he would not stand by and see free-born men
degraded against all right and justice, and protested
against our savage foeman's threats not only in word
but in act. His protests were seconded by his hired
servant and by one or two passengers,—very much
exhausted by sea-sickness, and whose interference was
more of an inducement to further violence than an
accession of strength. I asked for no mercy for myself, but shaking my fists in Tryphaena's face, I cried
out in a bold, loud voice, I would use all my strength
upon her, if she laid a finger on Giton, cursed woman
that she was, the only person in the ship that really
wanted flogging.

This insolence made Lichas still more angry, for
he was furious at seeing me thus abandon my own
cause to protest on Giton's behalf. Nor was Tryphaena less enraged at the affront, and the whole ship's
company was split into two opposing factions. On the
one side the barber servant is busied distributing his
razors amongst us, after first arming himself with one
of them, on the other Tryphaena's slaves are tucking
up their sleeves the better to use their fists. Even the
maids did their part, encouraging the combatants with
their cries, the pilot alone protesting and declaring he
would leave the helm, if they did not make an end of

this frantic uproar all about a couple of lecherous blackguards.

Even this threat failed to mitigate the fury of the disputants, our adversaries fighting for revenge, and ourselves for dear life. Numbers fall on either side, though no one is actually killed; still more retire wounded and bleeding, like soldiers after a pitched battle—without anyone showing the smallest loss of determination.

At this crisis the gallant Giton suddenly clapped his razor menacingly to his virile parts, threatening to amputate the cause of so many calamities; but Tryphaena forbade the perpetration of the horrid deed, readily granting him quarter. I myself repeatedly laid a similar weapon to my throat, though without any more intention of really killing myself than Giton had of carrying out his threat. At the same time he was able to enact the comedy with the more reckless realism, knowing as he did that the razor in his hand was the identical one he had once already cut his throat with.

Both sides kept the field with equal resolution, till the pilot, seeing it was likely to be no everyday fight, arranged after no little difficulty that Tryphaena should act as peacemaker and effect a truce. So after mutual pledges had been exchanged in the time-honoured fashion, holding forth an olive branch she had hastily snatched from the image of the tutelary deity of the vessel, she advanced boldly to the parley.

"What direful rage, she cries, turns peace to war?
What crime is ours? No faithless Paris here
Rides in our ship, nor Menelaus' bride,
Nor with a brother's gore Medea dyed.
'Tis slighted love inspires the feud, and craves
For blood and murderous deeds amidst these waves;
Why die before our time? your wrath forbear,
Nor make the harmless sea your passions share!"

This effusion, pronounced by Tryphaena in a broken voice, did something to stop the fray, the combatants at length turning their thoughts to a peaceful solution and ceasing from active hostilities. Eumolpus, the leader on our side, at once seized the opportunity for reconciliation thus offered, and after first indulging in a fierce invective against Lichas and all his doings, put his seal to a treaty of peace, which ran as follows:

"From the bottom of your heart, you, Tryphaena, do promise and undertake to forego all complaint of the wrong done you by Giton; and never by reason of any act of his committed aforetime, to upbraid, or punish, or in any wise molest him. Furthermore, that you will do nothing to the boy against his free will and pleasure, neither embracing, nor kissing, the said Giton, nor fornicating with him,—except under forfeiture of one hundred denars for such offence.

"Item: from the bottom of your heart, you, Lichas, do promise that you will in no wise annoy Encolpius with word or look of contumely, nor inquire where he may sleep at night; or if you so do, that you will incontinently count down two hundred denars for each offence."

A truce being agreed to upon these terms, we laid down our arms, and in order that no vestige of rancour might be left, once the oath was taken, it was resolved we should kiss away all memory of past injuries. All being unanimous for peace, our swelling passions soon subside, and a banquet served with emulous alacrity crowns our reconciliation with the pledge of good-fellowship. The whole ship resounds with singing, and a sudden calm having arrested her progress, one might be seen harpooning the fish that leapt above the waves, while another would be hauling in the struggling prey enticed by his cunningly baited hooks. Sea-birds too came and settled on the main-yard; these a practised sportsman touched with his jointed fowling-rods, and conveyed them glued to the limed tackle into our very hands. The down flew dancing in the air, while the larger feathers fell into the sea and tossed lightly to and fro on the foam-capped waves.

Lichas seemed already on the point of making it up with me, and Tryphaena was throwing the last drops of her wine amorously over Giton, when Eumolpus, who was as drunk as anybody, took it into his head to start jeering at people who were bald-headed and branded. Eventually coming to the end of his exceedingly pointless witticisms, he once more dropped into poetry, and treated us to the following little "Lament for Vanished Locks:"

Beauty is fallen! thy hair's soft vernal grace
To wintry baldness gives untimely place.
Thy injured temples mourn their ravished shade;
Waste, like a stubble field, thy brow is laid.
Fallacious gods! your treacherous gifts how vain!
You only give us joy, to give us pain.
Unhappy youth! but late thy curling gold
E'en Phoebus self might envy to behold;
But now for smoothness, nor the liquid air,
Nor watered pumpkin can with thee compare.
The laughter-loving maids you fly, and fear;
And death with hasty steps will soon be here.
His fatal night already clouds thy morn,
Beauty is fallen! and thy gay locks are shorn.

He was still longing, I verily believe, to give us
more of this stuff or perhaps something worse, when
Tryphaena's maid led Giton away below and dressed
the lad up in one of her mistress's heads of hair. She
next produced eyebrows out of a make-up box, and
cleverly following the lines of the lost features, soon
restored him to all his pristine comeliness. Tryphaena
saw Giton once more under his true colours, and bursting into tears, gave the boy the first genuine and
heartfelt kiss she had bestowed on him since his misfortunes. Rejoiced as I was to see the lad restored
to his former beauty, I could not help continually hiding my own face, feeling how extraordinarily I must
be disfigured, since Lichas did not deign to give me so
much as a word. However I was rescued before long
from these sad thoughts by the kind offices of the

same maid-servant, who now called me aside and decked me out with an equally elegant substitute for my lost ringlets. Indeed my face looked prettier than ever, as it happened to be a flaxen wig.

But Eumolpus, champion of the distressed and author of the existing harmony, for fear our cheerfulness should flag for lack of amusing anecdotes, commenced a series of gibes at women's frailty,—how lightly they fell in love, how quickly they forgot even their own sons for a lover's sake, asserting there was never yet a woman so chaste she might not be wrought to the wildest excesses by a lawless passion. Without alluding to the old plays and world-renowned examples of women's folly, he need only instance a case that had occurred, he said, within his own memory, which if we pleased he would now relate. This offer concentrated the attention of all on the speaker, who began as follows:

"There was once upon a time at Ephesus a lady of so high repute for chastity that women would actually come to that city from neighbouring lands to see and admire. This fair lady having lost her husband, was not content with the ordinary signs of mourning, such as walking with hair dishevelled behind the funeral car and beating her naked bosom in presence of the assembled crowd; she was fain further to accompany her lost one to his final resting-place, watch over his corpse in the vault where it was laid according to the Greek mode of burial, and weep day and night beside it. So deep was her affliction, neither family nor friends could dissuade her from these austerities and the purpose she had formed of perishing of hunger. Even the Magistrates had to retire worsted after a last but fruitless effort. All mourned as virtually dead already a woman of such singular determination, who had already passed five days without food.

"A trusty handmaid sat by her mistress's side, mingling her tears with those of the unhappy woman, and trimming the lamp which stood in the tomb as often as it burned low. Nothing else was talked of throughout the city but her sublime devotion, and men of every station quoted her as a shining example of virtue and conjugal affection.

"Meantime, as it fell out, the Governor of the Province ordered certain robbers to be crucified in close proximity to the vault where the matron sat bewailing the recent loss of her mate. Next night the soldier who was set to guard the crosses to prevent anyone coming and removing the robbers' bodies to give them burial, saw a light shining among the tombs and heard the widow's groans. Yielding to curiosity, a failing common to all mankind, he was eager to discover who it was, and what was afoot. Accordingly he descended into the tomb, where beholding a lovely woman, he was at first confounded, thinking he saw a ghost or some supernatural vision. But presently the spectacle of the husband's dead body lying there, and the woman's tear-stained and nail-torn face, everything went to show him the reality, how it was a disconsolate widow unable to resign herself to the death of her helpmate. He proceeded therefore to carry his humble meal into the tomb, and to urge the fair mourner to cease her indulgence in grief so excessive, and to leave off torturing her bosom with unavailing sobs. Death he declared was the common end and last home of all men, enlarging on this and the other commonplaces generally employed to console a wounded spirit. But the lady, only shocked by this offer of sympathy from a stranger's lips, began to tear her breast with redoubled vehemence, and dragging out handfuls of her hair, to lay them on her husband's corpse.

"The soldier however, refusing to be rebuffed, renewed his adjuration to the unhappy lady to eat. Eventually the maid, seduced doubtless by the scent of the wine, found herself unable to resist any longer, and extended her hand for the refreshment offered; then with energies restored by food and drink, she set herself to the task of breaking down her mistress's resolution. 'What good will it do you,' she urged, 'to die of famine, to bury yourself alive in the tomb, to yield your life to destiny before the Fates demand it?

" ' "Think you to pleasure thus the dead and gone?"

" 'Nay! rather return to life, and shaking off this womanly weakness, enjoy the good things of this world as long as you may. The very corpse that lies here before your eyes should be a warning to make the most of existence.'

"No one is really loath to consent, when pressed to eat or live. The widow therefore, worn as she was with several days' fasting, suffered her resolution to be broken, and took her fill of nourishment with no less avidity than her maid had done, who had been the first to give way.

"Now you all know what temptations assail poor human nature after a hearty meal. The soldier resorted to the same cajolements which had already been successful in inducing the lady to eat, in order to overcome her virtue. The modest widow found the young soldier neither ill-looking nor wanting in address, while the maid was strong indeed in his favour and kept repeating:

"Why thus unmindful of your past delight,
    Against a pleasing passion will you fight?"

"But why make a long story? The lady showed herself equally complaisant in this respect also, and the victorious soldier gained both his ends. So they lay together not only that first night of their nuptials, but a second likewise, and a third, the door of the vault being of course kept shut, so that anyone, friend or stranger, that might come to the tomb, should suppose this most chaste of wives had expired by now on her husband's corpse. Meantime the soldier, entranced with the woman's beauty and the mystery of the thing, purchased day by day the best his means allowed him, and as soon as ever night was come, conveyed the provisions to the tomb.

"Thus it came about that the relatives of one of the malefactors, observing this relaxation of vigilance, removed his body from the cross during the night and gave it proper burial. But what of the unfortunate soldier, whose self-indulgence had thus been taken advantage of, when next morning he saw one of the crosses under his charge without its body! Dreading instant punishment, he acquaints his mistress with what had occurred, assuring her he would not await the judge's sentence, but with his own sword exact the penalty of his negligence. He must die therefore; would she give him sepulture, and join the friend to the husband in that fatal spot?

"But the lady was no less tender-hearted than virtuous. 'The Gods forbid,' she cried, 'I should at one and the same time look on the corpses of two men, both most dear to me. I had rather hang a dead man on the cross than kill a living.' So said, so done; she orders her husband's body to be taken from its coffin and fixed upon the vacant cross. The soldier availed himself of the ready-witted lady's expedient, and next day all men marvelled how in the world a dead man had found his own way to the cross."

CHAPTER FOURTEEN

THIS story set the sailors all laughing, while it made Tryphaena blush not a little and lay her face amorously against Giton's bosom. Lichas on the other hand was far from laughing, and shaking his head indignantly, "If the Governor of Ephesus had been a just man," he declared, "he should have returned the good husband's body to the tomb and hung the woman on the cross." Doubtless he was thinking of the injury done to his own bed, and the pillage of his ship by the roving band of wantons. But not only did the terms of our treaty forbid his bearing rancour, but the mirth that filled all hearts left no room for resentment. Meantime Tryphaena, sitting on Giton's lap, was now covering his breast with kisses, now adjusting his wig so as to set off his face in spite of the loss of his ringlets.

For myself, so chagrined and impatient was I at this new and unexpected reconciliation I could neither eat nor drink, but sat looking grimly askance at the pair. Every kiss they exchanged wounded me, and every artful blandishment the wanton employed. I knew not whether I was the more incensed with the boy for having robbed me of my mistress, or with my mistress for debauching the boy. Both sights cut me to the quick, and were far more painful than my late captivity. To make things worse, Tryphaena never vouchsafed me a word, as she surely might have to a friend and a once favoured lover, nor did Giton deign so much as to do me the common courtesy of drinking my health, or at the very least speaking to me in the course of general conversation. I suppose he was afraid, just at the commencement of renewed favours on the lady's part, of re-opening a scarcely healed wound. Tears of vexation wetted my bosom, and the groans I stifled under the guise of a sigh all but choked me.

> The vulture grim that, sick hearts torturing,
>   Mangles the inmost vitals day and night,
> Is not the bird complacent poets sing,
>   But bitter jealousy and sore despite.

Notwithstanding my dismal countenance, my flaxen wig set off my beauty to advantage, and Lichas, inflamed afresh with amorousness, began to cast sheep's eyes at me and to solicit my favours, adopting more the tone of a friend than of a supercilious master who commands. Many were his attempts, but all in vain; at last, his advances meeting with nothing but decided rebuffs, his love changed to fury, and he endeavoured to carry the place by assault. But Tryphaena, making a sudden inroad, observed his naughtiness, whereupon he hurriedly adjusts his dress in great confusion, and takes to his heels.

This added fresh fuel to Tryphaena's wantonness, who demanded, "What was Lichas aiming at in these ardent attempts of his?" She forced me to explain.

and fired by my tale, remembering too our former intimate relations, would fain have had me renew our bygone amours. But I was tired out with excessive venery, and rejected her advances with scorn. At this, Tryphaena, in a frenzy of desire, threw her arms wildly around me and hugged me so tight I uttered a sudden cry of pain. One of the maids rushed in at the sound, and jumping to the conclusion I was extorting from her mistress the very favour I refused her, sprang at me and tore us apart. Mad with the disappointment of her lecherous passion, Tryphaena upbraided me violently, and with a thousand threats hastened away to Lichas, to still further exasperate him against me and to join him in contriving some means of vengeance.

You must know that at one time I had found much favour in this same waiting-maid's eyes, when I was on familiar terms with her mistress; so she took it extremely ill when she surprised me with Tryphaena, and sobbed bitterly. I eagerly inquired the reason of her distress, and after making some show of reluctance, she burst out, "If you have one drop of good blood in your veins, you will treat her as no better than a strumpet; as you are a man, don't go with that female catamite."

This incident perplexed my mind and made me still more anxious; but what I feared more than anything else was that Eumolpus might get wind of the circumstances, such as they were, and being a most sarcastic person might compose a versified lampoon to avenge my supposed wrongs, for in that case his fiery partizan-

ship would undoubtedly have made me ridiculous, a
thing I especially dreaded. I was just debating in my
own mind how I could keep Eumolpus from this knowl-
edge, when behold! the very man in question appeared,
perfectly acquainted with what had occurred; for Tryphaena had retailed the whole circumstances to Giton,
trying to indemnify herself for my rebuff at my little
favourite's expense. This had made Eumolpus furiously angry, all the more as these ebullitions of amorousness were open violations of the treaty signed and
sealed between us. The instant the old fellow set eyes
on me, he began bewailing my lot, and begged I would
tell him exactly how it had all happened. So I frankly
told him, seeing he was thoroughly posted already, of
Lichas's abominable attempt and Tryphaena's lecherous provocations. After listening to my tale, Eumolpus swore in good set terms, how he would most certainly avenge us, declaring the Gods were too just to
suffer such villainies to go unpunished.

Whilst we were still engaged in talk of this and the
like sort, the sea rose and heavy clouds gathering from
all quarters plunged the scene in darkness. The sailors run to their posts in panic haste, and take in sail
to ease the ship. But the wind, continually changing,
had raised a cross-sea, and the helmsman was uncertain what course to steer. At one moment the storm
would be driving us towards Sicily, while at others the
North Wind, that tyrant of the Italian coast, would
repeatedly whirl our helpless ship hither and thither
at its mercy; and what was more dangerous than all
the squalls, a sudden darkness had fallen, so think the

helmsman could not see even to the ship's bows. So the tempest being, God knows, utterly overpowering, Lichas stretches forth his hands towards me in terror and supplication, crying, "Help us, Encolpius, help us in our peril; restore that sacred robe and the sistrum you robbed the ship of. By all you hold sacred, have pity, you who are so tender-hearted usually." As he was vociferating thus, the gale swept him overboard; he rose once and again from the raging whirlpool, then the waters whirled him round and sucked him under.

Tryphaena on the contrary was saved by the fidelity of her slaves, who seized her, put her in ship's boat along with the greater part of her baggage, and so rescued her from certain death.

Clinging to Giton, I wept and cried, "Is all the Gods give us, to unite us only in death? Nay! cruel Fortune grudges even this. Look! in an instant the waves will overset the ship; look! the angry sea will in an instant sever the embraces of two lovers. If ever you truly loved Encolpius, kiss me, while you may, and snatch this last delight from swift impending doom."

As I said the words, Giton threw off his robe, and creeping inside my tunic, protruded his head to be kissed. Moreover, that the cruel waves might not tear our embrace asunder, he girt us both together with a girdle round our waists, crying, "If nothing else, at least we shall thus float longer united; or if the ocean be so merciful as to cast up our dead bodies on the same shore, either some passer-by will have the common humanity to heap a cairn over us, or else the unconscious sand will give us a burial even the angry waves cannot dispute." I submit to this last and final bond, and calm as if composed on my funeral couch, await a death I no longer dread.

The tempest meantime carries out the decrees of Fate, and beats down the last defences of the ship. Mast and rudder are carried away, and not a rope or an oar left; like a mere shapeless mass of logs she goes drifting with the billows. Some fishermen now put out hastily in their small craft to loot the vessel; but when they saw men were still on board ready to defend their property, they changed from wreckers into rescuers. Suddenly we hear an extraordinary noise, like the howling of a wild beast trying to get out, coming from underneath the master's cabin. Following up the sound, we discover Eumolpus seated, dashing down verses on a huge sheet of parchment. Marveling how the man could find leisure in the very face of death to be writing poetry, we haul him out in spite of his clamorous protests, telling him to have some common sense for once. But he was furious at the interruption, and shouted, "Let me finish my phrase; my poem's just in the throes of completion!" I laid violent hands on the maniac, calling on Giton to help me drag the bellowing poet ashore. After accomplishing our purpose with much difficulty, we found dismal shelter in a fisherman's hut, where having refreshed ourselves as best we might with provisions damaged by sea-water, we passed a most wretched night.

Next day, as we were debating what district we might most safely make for, I suddenly caught sight of a human body that was driving ashore, tossing lightly up and down on the waves. I stood sadly waiting, gazing with wet eyes on the work of the faithless element, and thus soliloquized, "Somewhere or another, mayhap, a wife is looking in blissful security for this poor fellow's return, or a son perhaps, or a father, all unsuspicious of storm and wreck; be sure, he has left some one behind, whom he kissed fondly at parting. This then is the end of human projects, this the accomplishment of men's mighty schemes. Look! how he rides the waves."

I was still deploring the stranger's fate, as I supposed him to be, when the swell heaved the face, still quite undisfigured, towards the beach, and I recognised the features of Lichas,—my erstwhile enemy, so formidable and implacable a foe, now cast helpless almost at my feet. I could restrain my tears no longer, but smiting my breast again and again, "Where is your anger now," I exclaimed, "and all your domineering ways? There you lie, a prey to the fishes and monsters of the deep; you who so short a while ago proudly boasted your despotic powers, have never a plank left of your great ship. Go to, mortals; swell your hearts with high-flown anticipations. Go to, ye men of craft; arrange the disposal for a thousand years to come of the wealth you have got by fraud. Why! only yesterday this dead man here cast up the accounts of his fortune, and actually fixed in his own mind the day, when he should return to his native shore. Ye Gods! how far away he lies from the point he hoped to reach. Nor is it the sea alone that disappoints men's hopes like this. The warrior is betrayed

by his arms; the householder in the act of paying his
offerings to heaven is overwhelmed in the ruin of his
own penates. One is thrown from his car, and breathes
his last hurried breath; the glutton dies of an over-
hearty meal, the frugal man of fasting. Reckon it
aright, and there is shipwreck everywhere. But then
a drowned man misses burial you object. As if it made
one scrap of difference how the perishable body is consumed,—by fire, by water, or by time. Do what you
will, these all end in the same result. Ah! but wild
beasts will mangle his corpse. As if fire would treat
it any kindlier; why! fire is the very penalty we deem
the most appalling, when we are savage with our
slaves. What folly then to make such ado to ensure
that no part of us remain unburied, when the Fates
arrange this matter at their pleasure, whether we will
or no."

After indulging in these grim thoughts, we proceed
to perform the last offices to the dead man, and Lichas,
borne by the hands of his ill-wishers to the pile, is
consumed to ashes. Eumolpus meantime is busy composing an epitaph for the departed, and after rolling
his eyes about for a while in search of inspiration, de-
livers himself of the following fragment:

. . . . His doom was sealed,
No carven marble marked his sepulture;
Five feet of common earth received the corpse,
His tomb a lowly mound. . . . .

This office duly and willingly performed, we pur-
sue our interrupted journey, and in a very brief space

of time arrive sweating at the top of a hill, from whence we spy at no great distance a city occupying the summit of a lofty crag. We did not know its name, being mere wanderers, until a peasant informed us it was Croton, a very ancient place and once upon a time the first town of all Italy. We next inquired anxiously what sort were the people inhabiting this famous site, and what commerce they mostly carried on since the ruin of their former prosperity by constantly recurring wars.

"Good strangers," the fellow replied, "if so be you are merchants, change your trade and seek some other means of livelihood. But if you are of a more genteel stamp, and can tell lies without end and stick to them, you're in the straight road to fortune. In this city literature is not cultivated, nor does eloquence find favour; sobriety and morality meet with neither commendation nor success; its inhabitants each and all, you must know, belong to one or other of two classes, viz. legacy hunters and their prey. In this city no man rears children, for whosoever has natural heirs of his own, is admitted to no entertainment, no public show; excluded from every privilege of citizenship, he is condemned to a life of furtive obscurity among the lowest of the low. The unmarried on the contrary and all who have no near kindred, attain the highest honours; they alone are brave, and capable, and respectable. You will find the town," he concluded, "like a pest-field, where two things are to be seen—corpses being torn, and crows tearing them."

Eumolpus, more far-seeing than the rest of us, pon-

dered over these novel arrangements and admitted the
method indicated of making a fortune took his fancy.
For my part, I supposed the old poet was joking in
his fantastic way, but he went on quite seriously, "I
only wish I had a more adequate stock in trade, I
mean a more fashionable robe and more elegant outfit
generally, to make the imposture more convincing.
Great Hercules; I would get done with my wallet for
good and all, and lead you all straight to wealth." On
this I promised him whatever he required, provided
the dress we used for our light-fingered work would
satisfy him; together with anything we had appro-
priated from Lycurgus's place. As for ready money,
this we might safely trust the Mother of the Gods to
provide.

"What hinders us then," cried Eumolpus, "to arrange our little comedy? Make me master, if you like
my plan." None of us ventured to disapprove a proj-
ect where we had nothing to lose. Accordingly, to
ensure the deception being faithfully kept up by all
concerned, we swore an oath in terms dictated by
Eumolpus,—to endure fire, imprisonment, stripes, cold
steel, and whatsoever else he might command us, in his
behalf. Like regular gladiators we vowed ourselves
most solemnly to our master, body and soul.

After completing the oath-taking, we salute our
master with pretended servility, and are instructed all
to tell the same tale,—how Eumolpus had lost a son,
a young man of prodigious eloquence and high promise; how consequently the poor old father had quitted
his native city, that the sight of his boy's clients and

companions and the vicinity of his tomb might not be
continually renewing his brief. This sad event, we
were to add, had been followed by a recent shipwreck,
which had cost him two million sesterces; that it was
not however so much the loss of the money which annoyed him as the fact that for want of a proper retinue
he could not fittingly keep up his rank. Further, that
he had thirty millions in Africa invested in landed
estates and securities, and such a host of slaves scattered up and down Numidia they could storm Car-
thage at a pinch. In accordance with this scheme, we
direct Eumolpus to cough a great deal, to have a weak
digestion at any rate, and in company to grumble at
every dish set before him; to be for ever talking about
gold and silver, and unproductive farms, and how
terribly barren land always was; also every day to sit
over accounts, and regularly once a month to add new
codicils to his will. And to make the farce quite complete, whenever he wished to call one of us, he was
to use the wrong name, plainly showing the master
was thinking of other servants no longer with him.

Matters being thus arranged, after praying the gods
for "good success and happy issue," as the phrase runs,
we set forward. But poor Giton could not stand his
unusual load; while Corax, Eumolpus's hired man, ob-
jecting strongly to his job, kept everlastingly dropping
his pack and cursing us for going too fast; he swore
he would either throw away his traps, or else make off
with the swag altogether. "Do you take me for a
beast of burden," he grumbled, "or a stone-ship? I
contracted for a man's work, not a dray-horse's! I'm

as much a freeman as you are, though my father did leave me a poor man." Not content with bad language, he kept lifting up his leg again and again, and filling the road with a filthy noise and a filthy stench. Giton only laughed at his impudence, and after each explosion gave a loud imitation of the noise with his mouth.

But even this did not hinder the poet from relapsing into his accustomed vein. "Many are the victims, my young friends," he began, "poetry has seduced! The instant a man has got a verse to stand on its feet and clothed a tender thought in appropriate language, he thinks he has scaled Helicon right off. Many others, after long practice of forensic talents, finally retreat to the tranquil calm of verse-making as to a blessed harbour of refuge, imagining a poem is easier put together than an argument all embroidered with scintillating conceits. But a mind of nobler inspiration is revolted by this flippancy; and no intellect that is not flooded with a mighty tide of learning, can either conceive or bring to birth a worthy poetic child. In diction, anything approaching commonness, if I may use the word, is to be avoided; a poet must choose words devoid of base associations, and hold to Horace's,

I hate and bid avaunt the vulgar herd.

Again, care should be exercised to avoid sentiments that stand out as mere excrescences on the framework of the main conception; let the fabric be as brilliant as it may, its colours must be ingrained in the stuff. I may instance Homer, and the Lyric poets, and our Roman Virgil, and Horace with his happy preciosity.

The rest, one and all, were blind to the true path to Parnassus, or if they did see it, were afraid to tread it.

"Look at that mighty subject, the Civil Wars; anyone attempting it, if not a man of the ripest scholarship, will sink under the burden. It is no question of a string of facts to be catalogued in verse, a task the Historian will perform far better; nay! rather must the untrammelled spirit be hurried along through a series of digressions and divine interventions and all the intricacies of myth and fable. The inspired frenzy of the bard should be more apparent than the tested pedantry of scrupulous precision. For example, see how you like this rapid sketch,—though indeed it has not yet received the final touches:

> Now haughty Rome reigned mistress of the Globe,
> Where'er the Ether shines with heavenly fires,
> Or Earth extends, or circling Ocean rolls.
> Yet still insatiate, her winged navies ploughed
> The burdened main, to each unplundered shore;
> For to the rich she bore immortal hate,
> And her own avarice still prepared her Fall.
> E'en former pleasures were beheld with scorn,
> As joys grown threadbare by too vulgar use.
> The soldier now admired th' Assyrian dye,
> And now th' Hesperian charmed his fickle pride.
> Numidia here the lofty roof sustained;
> There shone the honours of Serean looms;
> Arabia of her balmy sweets was spoiled;
> Yet still unquenched, the lust of ravage burned.
> Through Maurian wilds, and Ammon's distant reign,

Monsters were captived for our cruel sports.
The stranger tiger in his golden cage
Now crossed the main to press our friendly shore;
Whilst joyful Rome her monster entertained
With purple streams of her own kindred blood.

I blush to speak, I tremble to recite
Our Persian manners, and our curse of Fate!
From Youth they snatched the Man with cruel art,
Whilst Venus frowned o'er the retreating tide;
As if they thought to favour the deceit,
E'en Age itself would like that tide retire!
Nature was lost, and sought herself in vain.
Hence naught but lewd effeminacies please,
Soft curling hair, and wantonness of dress,
And all that can disgrace man's godlike form.
From Afric slaves and purple carpets come,
With citron tables, rich in golden stains,
Around whose costly, but dishonoured pride,
Buried in wine, the giddy drunkards lie.
Nothing escapes our raging lust of taste;
The soldier draws his sword in rapine's cause;
And from Sicilia's distant main the scar
Is brought alive to our luxurious board;
The Lucrine shore is of its oysters spoiled,
And hunger purchased with th' expensive sauce;
Phasis is widowed of its feathered race,
And nothing heard o'er all the desert strand
But trees remurmuring to the passing gales.

Nor less in Mars's Field Corruption swayed,
Where every vote was prostitute to gain;
The People and the Senate both were sold.

E'en Age itself was deaf to Virtue's voice,
And all its court to sordid interest paid,
Beneath whose feet lay trampled Majesty.
E'en Cato's self was by the crowd exiled.
Whilst he who won suffused with blushes stood,
Ashamed to snatch the power from worthier hands.
Oh! shame to Rome and to the Roman name!
'Twas not one man alone whom they exiled,
But banished Virtue, Fame and Freedom too.
Thus wretched Rome her own destruction bought,
Herself the merchant, and herself the ware.
Besides, in debt was the whole Empire bound,
A prey to Usury's insatiate jaws;
Not one could call his house, or self, his own;
But debts on debts like silent fevers wrought,
Till through the members they the vitals seized.

Fierce tumults now they to their succour call,
And War must heal the wounds of Luxury;
For Want may safely dare without a fear.
And sunk in hopeless misery, what could awake
Licentious Rome from her voluptuous trance,
But fire, and sword, and all the din of arms?
Three mighty chiefs kind Fortune had supplied,
Whom cruel Fate in various manner slew.
The Parthian fields were drunk with Crassus'
    gore;
Great Pompey perished on the Libyan main;
And thankless Rome saw greater Julius bleed.
Thus as one soil too narrow were to hold
Their rival dust, their ashes shared the World.
But their immortal glory never dies.

'Twixt Naples and Dicharchian fields extends
A horrid Gulf, immensely deep and wide,
Through which Cocytus rolls his lazy streams,
And poisons all the air with sulphurous fogs.
No Autumn here e'er clothes himself with green,
Nor joyful Spring the languid herbage cheers;
Nor feathered warblers chant their mirthful strains
In vernal comfort to the rustling boughs;
But Chaos reigns, and ragged rocks around
With naught but baleful cypress are adorned.

Amidst these horrors Pluto raised his head,
With mingled flames and ashes sprinkled o'er,
Stopped Fortune in her flight, and thus addressed:
Oh! thou whose sceptre Heaven and Earth
  controls!
Who had'st the power which too securely stands,
And only heap'st thy favours to resume;
Dost thou not sink beneath Rome's ponderous
  weight,
Unable to sustain her tottering pride?
E'en Rome herself beneath her burden groans.
And ill sustains Monopoly of Power.
For see elate in Luxury of Spoils,
Her golden domes invade the frighted skies!
Sea's turned to land, and land is turned to sea,
And injured Nature mourns her slighted Laws.
E'en me they threaten, and besiege my Throne;
The Earth is ransacked for her treasured stores,
And in the solid hills such caverns made,
That murmuring ghosts begin to hope for day.

Change, Fortune, therefore, change this prideful
    scene!
Fire every Roman's breast with civil rage,
And give new subjects to my desert reign!
For ne'er have I been joyed with human gore,
Nor my Tisiphone e'er quenched her thirst,
Since Sulla's sword let loose the purple tide,
And reaped the harvest of insatiate death.
    He spoke . . . . when straight the opening **Earth**
    disclosed,
And to the Goddess' hand his hand he joined.
Then Fortune, smiling, this reply addressed:
    Oh! Father who Cocytus' empire sways!
If dangerous truth may safely be revealed,
Enjoy your wish! not less my anger boils,
And in my breast as fierce resentment burns.
I hate the height to which I've lifted Rome,
And my own lavished favours now repent.
But that same God who built her haughty power,
Shall soon rehumble to the dust her pride.
Then I'll with transport light the general flame,
And with the plenteous slaughter feast revenge.
Methinks I see Thessalia's fatal plain
Already heaped with dead, and funeral piles
Innumerous blazing on Iberia's shore!
I see the Libyan sands distained with blood,
And sevenfold Nile groans with prophetic fears!
On every side the clang of arms resounds,
An Actium's flight seems present to my eyes!
Then open all the portals of thy Reign,
And give thy crowding subjects free access!

Old Charon in his boat can ne'er convey
The shoals of ghosts that for their passage wait,
But needs a fleet!—Tisiphone may then
Quench her dire thirst, and cloy herself with Fate.
The mangled World is hurrying to thy Reign.
 Scarce had she spoke, when from a sulphurous
   cloud
Blue lightnings flashed, and sudden thunders roared.
Affrighted Pluto feared his brother's darts,
And trembling hid his head in shades of night.
 The Gods by dreadful omens straight disclosed
The deathful horrors of approaching Fate.
The Sun in bloody clouds obscured his rays,
As if he mourned the dreadful scene begun;
Whilst trembling Cynthia fled the impious sight,
Quenching her orb, and from the World withdrew.
Mountains by sudden storms were overturned;
And erring rivers left their channels dry.
E'en Heaven itself confesses the alarm,
And fierce battalions skirmish in the clouds;
Etna redoubles all her sulphurous rage,
And darts strange lightnings at th' affrighted sky;
Unburied ghosts too wander round the tombs,
And with impatient threatenings ask repose;
A fiery comet shakes her blazing hair;
And wondering Jove descends in showers of blood.
Nor was it long that Heaven th' event concealed;
For mighty Caesar panting for revenge,
Gave peace to Gaul, and flew to Civil Arms.
 Upon the towering Alps' remotest height,
Where the cragg'd rocks look down upon the clouds,

A Grecian altar to Alcides smokes.
There everlasting Winter bars access,
And the ambitious summit props the skies;
No Summer ever darts his genial beams,
Nor vernal Zephyrs cheer the joyless air;
But snows on snows accumulated rise,
The icy pillars of the starry Orb.
Here Caesar with his joyful legions climbed;
Here camped; and from the lofty precipice,
Surveying all Hesperia's fertile plains.
With hands uplifted, thus addressed his prayer:
   Almighty Jove! and thou, Saturnian Earth,
So oft by me with filial triumphs graced!
Witness these arms I with reluctance bear,
Compelled by matchless wrongs to War's redress.
Proscribed and exiled, whilst the Rhine's proud flood
I swelled beyond its banks with native gore,
And to his Alps confined the haughty Gaul,
Once more to storm your Capitol prepared.
But what reward has all these toils repaid?
Conquest alas! is by herself undone!
Germania vanquished a new crime is deemed,
And sixty Triumphs are with exile crowned.
But what are they my glory thus compels
To count the aid of mercenary arms?
Oh! shame to Rome! My Rome disowns their birth
Nor shall they long her injured honours stain,
Beneath this arm their envious Chief shall fall!
Come fellow-victors, rouse your martial rage,
And with your conquering swords assert my cause!
One is our danger, and our crime the same.

It was not I alone reaped glory's field,
But thanks to you! by you these laurels won;
Then since disgrace and punishment's decreed,
Mutual our trophies and victorious toils,
The die be thrown! and Fortune judge the cast!
Let each brave warrior grasp his shining blade!
For me my rights already crowned appear,
Nor 'midst so many heroes doubt success.

    He spoke, . . . when swift-descending from the
       Sky,
The Bird of Jove urged his auspicious flight.
Strange voices in the left-hand woods were heard;
And issuing flames flashed through the sylvan
       gloom.
Phoebus himself assumed his brightest beams,
And with unusual splendour cheered the day.

    Fired with the omen, dauntless Caesar bids
His engines move; himself the first t' essay
The dangerous path; for yet in frost confined
And peaceful horrors lay the passive ground.

    But when with ardent feet th' innumerous train
Of men and horse and icy fetters loosed,
To fierce resistance swelled the melted snows,
And sudden rivers o'er the mountains rolled.
But soon again as if by Fate's command,
The rising waves in icy billows stood;
Whilst in confusion o'er the treacherous path
Horses and men and mingled standards lay.
To aid the horror, sudden winds compel
The gathering clouds, and burst into a storm,
Thick o'er their ringing arms and hail descends,

And from the Ether pours an icy sea;
One common ruin conquers Earth and Sky,
And frighted rivers hurry o'er their banks;
But dauntless Caesar aided by his spear,
Still presses forward with unshaken soul.
  With such an ardour was Alcides fired,
When down Caucasian steeps he rushed to fame.
And thus descending from Olympus' brow,
Almighty Jove the Giants put to flight.
  Meantime on trembling pinions through the Skies
To Mount Palatium frighted Rumour flew,
And to astonished Rome these tidings bore:
A hostile Fleet is riding on the main,
And o'er the Alps, with German conquests flushed,
The vengeful Legions pour on guilty Rome.
Straight Fire and Sword and all the dreadful train
Of civil rage before their eyes appear!
Distracting tumults every bosom swayed,
And Reason 'midst the dubious fears was lost.
This flies by land, and that confides the sea,
As far less dangerous than his native shores!
These run to arms; Fate aids the wild affright,
And each obeys the guidance of his fears.
No certain course the giddy vulgar know,
But through the Gates in thronged confusion crowd,
And rival terror;—Rome to Rumour yields,
And weeping Romans leave their native seats.
This is his hand his trembling children leads,
And this his gods within his bosom hides,
His long-loved threshold quits with mournful looks,
And wings his curses at the absent foe.

There on the husband's breast the bride complains;
And here his father's age a pious youth
Supports with filial care, nor feels his load,
Nor fears but for his venerable charge.
Whilst these, insensate! to the field convey
Their treasured wealth, and glut the war with spoils.

As on the deep when stormy Auster blows,
And mounts the billows with tumultuous rage,
Th' affrighted seamen ply their arts in vain;
The pilots stand aghast; these lash their sails;
Whilst these make land, and those avoid the shores,
And rather Fortune than the rocks confide.

But what can paint the fears that seized each
  breast,
When both the Consuls with great Pompey fled?
Pompey, Hydaspes' and proud Pontus' scourge,
The rock of Pirates, whom with wonder Jove
Had thrice beheld in the triumphal Car!
That mighty Chief who gave the Euxine laws,
And taught th' admiring Bosphorus to obey,
Oh shame! deserted the Imperial Name,
And meanly left both Rome and Fame behind!
Whilst fickle Fortune gloried in his flight.

The Gods with horror see th' intestine jars,
And even celestial breasts consent to fear.
For see the mild pacific train depart.
Exiled the World by our impiety!
First soft-winged Peace extends her snowy arm,
And pulling o'er her brows her olive wreath,
Seeks the Elysian shades with hasty flight.
On her with downcast eyes meek Faith attends,

And mourning Justice with dishevelled hair,
And weeping Concord with her garments rent.

But joyful Hell unbolts the brazen doors,
And all her Furies quit the Stygian Court.
Threatening Bellona with Erinys joins,
And dire Megaera armed with fiery brands.
Pale Death, insidious Fraud, and Massacre,
With Rage, burst forth! Who from his fetters freed,
Lifts high his gory head; a helmet hides.
His wounded visage, and his left hand grasps
The shield of Mars horrid with countless darts.
Whilst in his right a flaming torch appears,
To light Destruction, and to fire the World.

The Gods descending also left the skies,
Whilst wondering Atlas missed his usual load;
And mortal jars even Heaven itself divide.
In Caesar's cause Dione first appeared;
Her Pallas aided, and the God of War.
Whilst in espousal of brave Pompey's part
Cynthia and Phoebus and Cyllene's son
And his own model, great Alcides, joined.
The trumpets sound! When straight fell Discord
    raised
Her Stygian head, and shook her matted locks.
With clotted blood her face was covered o'er,
And gummy horrors from her eyes distilled;
Two rows of cankered teeth deformed her mouth,
And from her tongue a stream of poison flowed;
Whilst hissing serpents played around her cheeks;
Her livid skin with rags was scarce concealed,
And in her trembling hand a torch she shook.

Ascending thus from the Tartarean gloom,
She reached the top of lofty Apennine;
Whence viewing all the subject land and sea,
And armies floating on the crowded plains,
Thus into words her joyful fury broke:
   Now, rush ye Nations, rush to mutual arms,
And let Dissension's torch for ever burn!
For flight no longer shall the Coward save,
Nor age, nor sex, nor children's pity move,
But the Earth tremble, and her haughtiest towers
Shake in convulsive ruins to the ground.
Do thou, Marcellus, the Decree uphold;
And Curio, thou excite the madding crowd!
Nor thou, persuasive Lentulus, forbear
To aid the Faction with thy potent tongue!
But why, O Caesar, this delayed Revenge?
Why burst'st thou not the Gates of guilty Rome,
And mak'st her treasured pride thy welcome prey?
And thou, great Pompey, know'st thou not thy
      power?
If thou fear'st Rome, to Epidamnus haste,
And feast Thessalia's plain with human gore!
   Thus Discord spoke, . . . the impious Earth
   obeyed.

CHAPTER FIFTEEN

Eumolpus having declaimed this effusion with prodigious volubility, we eventually entered the gates of Croton. Here we baited at a small, mean inn, but started out next morning to find a lodging of greater pretensions. We soon fell in with a mob of legacy hunters, who plied us with questions as to who we were and where we came from. So we answered both enquiries, in strict accordance with the plan arranged between us, with an exaggerated glibness, and they believed every word of it; for they instantly put their fortunes at Eumolpus's disposal, almost fighting which should be first to do him this service. One and all offer presents, in order to curry favour with the supposed millionaire.

Things went on thus at Croton for a long time, till Eumolpus, intoxicated with success, so completely forgot his former lowly condition as to boast to his followers how no one could resist his influence, and that any misdemeanour they might have committed in the town, they could carry off with impunity by his friends' good offices. For my own part however, though every day I stuffed my swollen carcass with a greater superfluity of good things and really thought Fortune had at last ceased watching me with an eye of malevolence, still I often reflected on my present mode of life and the way it had come about. "What if some astute legacy hunter," I often said to myself, "sent some one to Africa to make enquiries, and discovered our swindle? What if Eumolpus's servant, as is just possible, sick of this life of luxury, should give a hint to his cronies and betray the whole imposture out of malice? Why! we should just have to fly once more, return to the penury we have at last got the better of, and start begging afresh. Gods and goddesses of heaven! what a life outlaws lead,—forever dreading the penalty of one felony or another!"

Thus communing with myself, I quit the house in a most melancholy mood, hoping to refresh my spirits with the open air out of doors. I had scarcely entered the public promenade, when a girl of far from unpleasing exterior met me, and calling "Polyaenos," the name I had adopted by way of disguise, informed me that her mistress desired permission to speak with me.

"You have surely made a mistake," I answered in some confusion; "I am but a foreigner and a slave, and quite undeserving of the honour."

"Nay! my mission was to yourself," she returned; "but I see, because you know your own beauty, you give yourself airs, and sell your favours, instead of giving them. What else can those waved and well combed locks mean, and that made-up face, and the languishing look of your eye, For what else that studied gait, and mincing steps that never exceed a measured pace, except to sell your person by the meretricious display of your charms? Look at me; I am no augur, no student of the planets like the astrologers, yet I can infer a man's character from his looks, and foretell his intentions the moment I see his way of walking. Therefore, if you are willing to sell us what I require, there's a customer all ready; or, if you will give it, like a gentleman, we shall be glad to be under this obligation to you. You tell me you are a slave and a common varlet; this only the more inflames my mistress's heated imagination. There are women fancy muck, whose passions are stirred only at the sight of slaves or runner boys with bare legs. Others are hot after gladiators, or dusty muleteers, or actors swaggering on the boards. This is the sort my mistress is; she jumps clean over the fourteen rows from orchestra to gallery, to seek her choice among the rabble of the back benches."

So, charmed with her fascinating chatter, "Tell me, my dear," I said, "is this lady who loves me yourself?" The maid laughed heartily at my cool way of putting it, saying, "Pray! pray! don't be so mighty pleased with yourself. I've never given myself to a slave yet; and god forbid I should waste my embraces on gallows-birds. 'Tis their own lookout, if ladies go kissing the marks the lash has left; for my part, though I'm only a servant maid, I never go with anybody below a knight.

"Tastes differ 'tis as chance disposes;
    Some like thorns, and some like roses."

I was astounded at such abnormal predilections, and thought it monstrous thus to find the maid with the mistress's fastidiousness, the mistress with the maid's vulgar tastes.

Presently, after further pleasantries had passed, I begged the girl to bring her mistress into the plane-tree avenue. She was quite agreeable, and tucking up her skirts dived into a laurel wood that bordered the promenade. In a very few moments she brought out her mistress from where she was hiding, and led her up to me, a more perfect being than ever artist fash-ioned. There are no words to express her beauty, for anything I can say will fall far short of the reality. Her locks, which curled naturally, rippled all over her shoulders, her brow was low, the hair being turned back from it, her brows, extending to the very spring of the cheek, almost met between the eyes, which shone brighter than stars in a moonless sky, her nose was slightly aquiline, her little mouth such as Praxiteles gave Diana. Chin, neck, hands, snow-white feet con-fined in elegant sandals of gold work, all vied with Parian marble in brilliancy. For the first time I thought lightly of Doris, whose long-time admirer I was.

Why tarries Jove, scorning the arts of Love,
Mute and inglorious in the heavens above?
How well the Bull would now the God become,
Or his gray hairs to be transformed to down!
Here's Danae's self,—a touch from her would fire,
And make the God in liquid joys expire.

Quite delighted, she smiled so sweetly I thought I saw the moon breaking full-faced from a cloud. Presently, with fingers punctuating her words, she laughed, "If you are not too proud to enjoy a woman of condition, and one who only within the year has known your sex, I offer you a 'sister', fair youth. You have a 'brother' already, I know, for I did not disdain to make enquiries, but what hinders you to adopt a sister too? I claim a like dignity. Only taste and try, when you will, how you like my kisses."

"Nay!" I replied, "by your own loveliness I abjure you, deign to admit an alien among your worshippers. You will find him a sincere devotee, if you give him leave to adore you. And that you may not think I enter this temple of Love giftless, I will sacrifice my 'brother' to you."

"What!" she cried, "you sacrifice to me the being you cannot live without, on whose kisses your happiness depends, whom you love as I would have you love me?" As she said these words, such a sweetness was you might have thought it was the Siren's harmonies came floating on the breeze. So, lost in admiration and dazzled with a wondrous effulgence brighter than the light of heaven, I was fain to ask my divinity's name.

"Why! did not my maid tell you," she replied, "I was called Circe? I am not indeed the daughter of the Sun; nor did my mother ever stay at her good pleasure the course of the revolving globe. Still I have one noble boon to thank heaven for, if the fates unite us two. Yes! some god's mysterious, silent workings are beneath all this. 'Tis not without a cause Circe loves Polyaenos; a great torch of sympathy flames between

these names. Then take your will of me. We have
no prying interference to dread; your 'brother' is far
away."

With these words Circe threw her arms, that were
softer than down, around my neck, and drew me down
on the flower-bespangled grass:

> On Ida's top, when Jove his nymph caressed,
> And lawless heat in open view expressed,
> His mother Earth in all her charms was seen,
> The rose, the violet, the sweet jessamine,
> And the fair lily smiling on the green.
> Such was the plat whereon my Venus lay;
> Our Love was secret, but the charming day
> Was bright, like her, and as her temple gay.

Side by side on the grass we lay, dallying with a
thousand kisses, the prelude to robuster joys. But
alas! a sudden debility of my nerves quite disappointed
Circe, who exclaimed, infuriated at the affront, "What
now? do my kisses revolt you? is my breath offensive
with fasting? are my armpits uncleanly and smelling?
If it is nothing of this sort, are you afraid of Giton?"

Flushing hotly at her words, I lost any little vigour
still left me, and my whole frame feeling dislocated, I
besought my mistress, "Do not, my Queen, aggravate
my misery. I am bewitched."

So trivial an excuse was far from appeasing Circe's
indignation. She turned her eyes contemptuously away
from me, and glancing towards her maid, "Tell me,
Chrysis," she said, "and tell me true. Am I repulsive?
am I sluttish? is there some natural blemish disfigures

my beauty? Do not deceive your mistress; there must be something strangely amiss about us."

Then, as Chrysis stood silent, she snatched up a mirror, and after rehearsing all the looks and smiles lovers are wont to exchange, she shook out her robe that lay crumpled on the ground, and flounced off into the Temple of Venus. I was left standing like a convicted felon, or a man horror-struck with some awful vision, asking myself whether the bliss I had been cheated of was indeed a reality or only a dream.

As when in sleep our wanton Fancy sports,
And our fond eyes with hidden riches courts,
We hug the theft; the smiling treasure fills
Our guilty hands; the conscious sweat distils;
Whilst labouring fear sits heavy on the mind,
Lest the big secret should an utterance find.
But when with night th' illusive joys retreat,
And our eyes open to the gay deceit,
That which we ne'er possessed, as lost, we mourn,
And for imaginary blessings burn.

My calamity really seemed to me a dream, or rather a hallucination; and so long did my enervation last, I could not so much as get up off the ground. However the mind recovering its tone by degrees, my strength slowly came back to me, and I made for home, where feigning indisposition, I threw myself down on my pallet. Before long, Giton, who had heard I was ill, entered my chamber in much concern. To make his mind easier, I told him I had gone to bed merely to take a rest, talking a deal of other stuff besides, but

not a word about my misadventure, as I very much
dreaded his jealousy. So to avoid all suspicion, drawing him to my side, I tried to give him a proof of my
love, but all my panting and sweating was in vain. He
got up full of indignation, and upbraiding me with
debilitated vigour and diminished affection, declared he
had noticed for a long time I must certainly have been
expending my strength of mind and body elsewhere.

"No! no! darling," I interrupted, "my affection for
you has always been the same; but reason now prevails
over love and lechery."

"Well! thank you, thank you for the Socratic inno-
cency of your passion. Alcibiades was not more un-
contaminated when he lay in his preceptor's bed." "I
tell you, little brother," I went on, "I have lost all
knowledge and sense of manhood. Dead and buried
that part of me that once made me a very Achilles!"

Seeing I was really unnerved, and afraid, if he
were caught alone with me, it might give rise to scan-
dal, he withdrew in haste, retreating to an inner room
of the house. He was hardly gone when Chrysis entered my room and handed me her mistress's tablets,
on which was written the following letter:

"Circe to Polyaenos—Greeting.

"If I were a mere wanton, I should complain of my
disappointment. Instead I am positively grateful to
your impotence; for so I enjoyed longer dalliance with
the semblance of pleasure. What I ask is, how you do,
and whether you got home on your own legs; for doctors say a man cannot walk without nerves. I will tell

you what I think; beware, young Sir, of paralysis. I never saw a patient in more imminent danger; upon my word and honour, you are as good as dead already. If a like lethargy attack your knees and hands, you may send straight for the undertaker's men.

"Well! well! dire as is the affront I have received, still I will never grudge a prescription to a man in your miserable plight. If you would be cured, ask Giton's help. You will recover your nerve, I assure you, if you sleep three nights running apart from your 'little brother.' For myself, I have no fear but I can find another admirer to love me a little. My mirror and my reputation both tell me this is true.

Farewell, (if you can)."

As soon as Chrysis saw I had read this caustic epistle to the end, "These accidents are common enough," she said, "and particularly in this city, where there are women can lure down the moon out of the sky. So never fear, your matter shall be set right; only write back graciously to my mistress and restore her confidence with a candid and gently-worded reply. For to tell you the honest truth—from the hour you wronged her, she has not been her own woman."

I complied very willingly with the girl's suggestion, and wrote the following answer on the tablets:

"Polyaenos to Circe—Greeting.

"I confess, Lady, I have often offended; I am but a man, and a young one still. But never before this day have I done mortal sin. The criminal admits his crime; any penalty you inflict, I have richly deserved. I have betrayed a trust, slain a man, violated a temple; assign due punishment for all these crimes. If you choose to kill me, I hand you my sword; if you are satisfied with stripes, I haste to throw myself naked at my mistress's feet. Remember one thing only, 'twas not myself, but my tools that failed me. The soldier was ready but he had no arms. What so demoralized me, I cannot tell. Perhaps my imagination outran my lagging powers, perhaps in my all-aspiring eagerness, I lavished by ardour prematurely. I know not how it was. You bid me beware of paralysis; as if a greater palsy could exist than that which robbed me of the power to possess you. But this is the sum and substance of my plea; I will satisfy you yet, if you will grant me leave to repair my fault."

After dismissing Chrysis with fair promises of this sort, I put my body, which had served me so ill, into special training, and pretermitting the bath together, restricted myself to a moderate use of unguents. Then adopting a more fortifying diet, that is to say onions and snails' heads without sauce, I also cut down my wine. Finally composing my nerves by an easy walk before retiring, I went to bed with no Giton to share my couch. For anxious as I was to make my peace, I was afraid of even the slightest contact with my favourite.

Next day, having risen sound in mind and body, I went down to the same plane-tree walk, though truly I felt a dread of the ominous locality, and waited for Chrysis to act as my guide. After strolling to and fro for a while, I had just sat down in the same spot as the day before, when she came in sight, bringing a little old woman with her. When she had saluted me, "How now, Sir Squeamish," she began, "do you feel yourself in better fettle?"

The old woman meantime drew from her pocket a hank of plaited yarns of different colours, and tied it round my neck. Then puddling dust and spittle together, she dipped her middle finger in the mess, and disregarding my repugnance, marked my forehead with it.

Never despair; Priapus I invoke,
To help the parts that make his altars smoke.

The incantation ended, she bade me spit out thrice, and thrice toss pebbles into my bosom, which she had wrapped up in purple after pronouncing a charm over them. Then putting her hands to my privates, she began to try my virile condition. Quicker than thought the nerves obeyed her summons, and filled the old lady's hand with a huge erection. Then jumping for joy, "Look, Chrysis, look," she cried, "how I've started the hare for other folks to course." This accomplished, the old woman handed me back to Chrysis, who was overjoyed at the recovery of his mistress's treasure; with all haste she led me straight to the latter, whom we found in a most delightful spot, quite retired and adorned with everything of fairest Nature can show to charm the eyes.

Where noble Planes cast a refreshing shade,
And well-trimmed Pines their shaking tops
    displayed,
And Daphne midst the Cypress crowned her head.
Near by a circling river gently flows,
And rolls the pebbles as it murmuring goes.
A spot designed for Love; the nightingale
And gentle swallow its delights can tell,
Who on each bush salute the coming day,
And in their orgies sing its hours away.

She lay luxuriously stretched on golden cushions,
which supported her marble neck, fanning the calm
air with a branch of flowering myrtle. Directly she
saw me, she blushed a little, no doubt remembering
yesterday's affront; presently, when we were quite
alone, and at her invitation I had sat down by her side,
she laid the branch over my eyes, and this embolden-
ing her as if a wall had been raised between us, "How
goes it, paralytic?" she laughed, "are you quite recovered, that you've come back again to-day?"

"Why ask me," I returned, "instead of making
trial?" and throwing myself bodily into her arms, I
took my fill of good, healthy, unbewitched kisses. Her
loveliness drew me irresistibly to her and disposed me
to enjoyment. Already had our lips joined in many
a sounding kiss, our fingers interlocked had played all
sorts of amorous pranks, our two bodies had twined
in mutual embraces till our very souls seemed fused
in one; yet in the very height of these delicious pre-
liminaries, lo! my nerves once more betrayed me, and

I failed utterly to reach the supreme moment of our bliss.

Lashed to fury by two such dire affronts, the lady ends by seeking vengeance, and summoning her chamberlains, orders me a sound thumping. Not content with this cruel treatment of me, she calls together all the spinning wenches and meanest drudges of the house, and bids them spit at me. Clapping my hands to my eyes, and without one word of expostulation, for I knew I richly deserved it all, I fled from the house, driven forth under a hurricane of blows and spittle. Proselenos is kicked out too, and Chrysis beaten. The whole household was in dismay, all grumbling together and asking who it was had put their mistress in so vile a temper. This was some compensation and encouragement to me, and I carefully hid the marks of the blows I had received, not to make Eumolpus merry over my disaster, or Giton sad for the same reason. The only thing I could do to save my dignity was to pretend to be ill; this I did, and creeping into bed, turned the whole fire of my wrath against the vile cause of all my calamities:

> With dreadful steel the part I would have lopped;
> Thrice from my trembling hand the razor dropped.
> Now, what I might before, I could not do;
> For, cold as ice, the shuddering thing withdrew,
> And shrank behind a wrinkled canopy.
> Hiding its head from my revenge and me.
> Thus by its fear I'm baulked of my intent,
> And in mere mouthing words my anger vent.

So raising myself on my elbow, I addressed the recreant in some such terms as these, "What have you to say for yourself, abomination of gods and men? For indeed your very name must not be mentioned by self-respecting folks. Did I merit such treatment from you,—to be dragged down from heaven's bliss to hell's torments, to have the prime and vigour of my years maligned and to be reduced to the imbecility of dotage? Give me, I beseech you give me, a proof you are yet good for something." In words such as these I vented my irritation.

But with averted eyes, unmoved he mourned,
Nor to my fond reproach one look returned;
Like bended osiers trembling o'er a brook,
Or wounded poppies by no zephyr shook.

Nevertheless, on reaching the end of this undignified expostulation, I began to be ashamed of what I had been saying, and to blush furtively at having so far forgotten my self-respect as to bandy words with a part of my person men of graver sort do not so much as deign to notice. Presently after rubbing my brow awhile, "After all, what have I done so much amiss," I asked myself, "in thus relieving my resentment by means of a little natural abuse? Do ye not habitually curse various parts of our bodies, our belly, throat,— head even, when it aches, as it often does? Does not Ulysses quarrel with his own heart? and do not our Tragedians rail at their own eyes, as if they could hear? The gouty abuse their feet, the rheumatic their hands, the sore-eyed their optics; and does not a man who has damaged his toes, vent all the agony of his pain on his poor feet?"

Why do the solemn Catos of the Age
At my familiar lines unjustly rage?
In measures loose and plain blunt Satire flows,
And every Vice in proper colours shows.
Love I describe, and all the wanton joys
Of blushing matrons and of amorous boys.
Thus Epicurus taught: the Powers above
Regardless of terrestrial crimes below,
Enjoy a long Eternity of Love,
Letting the giddy World at random go.

Nothing is falser than mankind's silly prejudices, or sillier than an affectation of peculiar gravity.

CHAPTER SIXTEEN

My declamation ended, I called Giton to me and
asked him, "Tell me, darling, tell me on your honour;
that night Ascyltos stole you from me, did he resort
to active violence upon you, or was he content with
a night of self-restraint and continence?" The lad
touched his eyes, and swore in the most solemn terms
that Ascyltos had done him no harm. The truth is,
I was so crushed by my misfortunes I was not master
of myself, and did not rightly know what I was saying.
Let bygones be bygones, I said to myself, especially
when nothing but pain can come from recalling them.
Eventually I directed all my attention to the task of
recovering my lost vigour. I was ready even to devote
myself to the gods; accordingly I started out to implore
the help of Priapus. To make the best of things, I
feigned a cheerful countenance, and dropping on my
knees at the Temple threshold besought the deity's
intervention in the following lines:

"Delight of Bacchus, Guardian of the Groves,
The kind Restorer of decaying Loves,
Lesbos and verdant Thasos thee implore,
Whose maids thy power in wanton rites adore;
Joy of the Dryads, with propitious care
Attend my wishes, and indulge my prayer.

My guiltless hands with blood I never stained,
Or sacrilegiously the gods profaned;
Thus low I bow; restoring blessings send,
I did not thee with my whole self offend,
Who sins through weakness is less guilty thought;
Indulge my crime, and spare a venial fault.
When kindly Fate shall genial gifts allow,
I'll, not ungrateful, to thy godhead bow.
A suckling pig I'll offer at thy shrine,
And sacred bowls brim-full of generous wine;
A destined goat shall on thy altars lie,
And the horned parent of my flock shall die.
Then thrice thy frantic votaries shall round
Thy temple dance, with smiling garlands crowned,
And most devoutly drunk, thy Orgies sound."

Whilst I was thus engaged, anxiously intent on the part affected, the old woman entered the shrine with dishevelled hair and wearing black garments all in a state of disorder, and laying her hand on my shoulder led me outside the vestibule.

"What foul witches have devoured your manhood?" she exclaimed; "what refuse or what garbage have you trod on in the streets at night? You could not so much as do your duty by the boy; but flabby, faint and weary, like a cart-horse at a hill, you wasted your labour and your sweat in vain! And now, not content with your own delinquencies, you have set the gods against me as well—and I mean to make you smart for it."

So she led me unresisting back again into the Temple

and to the Priestess's chamber, where she pushed me down on the bed, and snatching up a cane that hung behind the door, she gave me yet another thrashing. Still I said not a word, and if the cane had not split at the first stroke, and so lessened the force of her blows, she would likely have broken my arms or my head. I groaned dismally, particularly at the way she worked my member, and bursting into a torrent of weeping, hid my face in my hands and cowered down on the pillow. The old woman was also melted to tears, and sitting down on the other side of the bed, began to complain in quavering tones of the tediousness of having lived too long.

Presently the Priestess came in. "Why! what has brought you to my chamber," she cried, "and with these long faces, as if you were come to a funeral? and on a holiday too, when even the most sorrow-laden laugh for once."

"Oh! it's this young man here, Œnothea," the old woman answered; "for sure, he was born under an evil star; he cannot sell his goods to boy or girl. You never saw so unfortunate a fellow; soaked leather, that's what his tool is! What think you of a man, I ask you that, who left Circe's bed without having tasted pleasure?" On hearing this, Œnothea sat down between us, and after shaking her head a while, "I am the only woman," she said, "knows how to cure this complaint. And that you may not think I'm doing at random, I require the young fellow to sleep one night with me, and see if I don't make it as stiff as horn!

"All Nature's works my magic power obey,
The blooming Earth shall wither and decay,
And when I please, be verdant, fresh and gay.
Here flowery vales shall vernal beauties know,
There frozen plains shall hide themselves in snow;
By magic charms I'll make a whirlwind cease,
Contract its breath, and murmur into peace;
Tigers and pards, submissive to my will,
Obey my orders and neglect to kill;
At my commands substantial darkness soon
O'erspreads the skies and hides the silver moon;
Sol's fiery car stops in th' Etherial plain,
And Thetis long expects her Lord in Vain.
The Pontic bulls emitting fire and smoke
The witch Medea to her service broke,
And made their swelling chest sustain her yoke.
Refulgent Circe, daughter of the Sun,
Could into swine Ulysses' soldiers turn;
In woods Silenus, Proteus in the seas,
Conceal the God, and take what form they please.
As great's my skill, as far my power extends,
The servile World to my enchantment bends."

I shuddered with terror to hear her promise such
miracles, and began to scrutinize the old woman more
carefully.

"Now," ejaculated Œnothea, "now do as I tell you."
And after washing her hands with scrupulous care, she
bent over the couch and kissed me again and again.

She then placed an old table on the middle of the
altar, and filling it with live coals, proceeded to patch

up an ancient bowl, so time-worn it was falling to pieces, with melted pitch. Next she put back in the smoke-begrimed wall a peg which had come down along with the wooden bowl, when she unhitched the latter. Presently after donning a square cloak, she set a huge cooking-pot on the fire, at the same time with a fork reaching down a cloth from the meat-rack, in which was stored a supply of beans and some exceedingly stale pieces of pig's cheek, slashed with a thousand cuts. She undid the string, shook out some of the contents on to the table, and bade me strip them smartly. Obeying her orders, I proceeded carefully to separate the beans from the filthy pods that contained them. But Œnothea, chiding my slowness, incontinently snatches them from me, and instantly stripping off the husks with her teeth, spits them out on the ground, where they looked like dead flies. I could not help admiring the ingenuity of poverty, and the knack there is in every single thing. Indeed this virtue of poverty found so ardent a follower in the priestess, it was conspicuous in every trifle about her. Her cottage especially was a very shrine of misery.

No Indian ivories here are set in gold,
No marble covers the deluded mould;
Void of expensive art, the reverent Shrine
With natural modest ornaments doth shine.
Round Ceres' bower the bending osier grows;
Earthen is all the plate the Priestess knows;
The jug is earth which holds the holy wine,
Osier the dish, sacred to Powers divine;

No brazen gauds are here, no purple pride,
Mud and dirt mixed the pious relics hide;
Rushes and reeds the humble roof adorn,
And straw deprived of its Autumnal corn.
On an old shelf a savoury ham is found,
And service-berries into garlands bound.
Such a low cottage Hecate confined,
Low was her dwelling, but sublime her mind.
Her bounteous heart a grateful praise shall crown,
And Muses make immortal her renown.

Then, having shelled the beans and eaten a scrap of
the meat, she took a fork and went to replace the pig's
cheek, which was as great an antiquity as herself; but
the rotten stool, on which she had mounted so as to
reach up to the rack, broke down under the old
woman's weight and threw her on the fire. The lip
of the cooking-pot was smashed, and put out the fire,
that was just burning up; the woman's elbow was burnt
by a red-hot ember, and her whole face begrimed
with the flying ashes. I sprang up in dismay, and not
without some inward laughter set the old thing on her
legs again; this accomplished, she ran instantly to a
neighbour's to replenish the fire, that nothing might
delay the sacrifice.

I was making my way to the door of the cottage,
when lo! and behold, three sacred geese, which I suppose the old woman was in habit of feeding at midday,
rushed at me and set me all in a twitter, pressing
round me with their disconcerting and almost rabid
cackle. One of them tore my tunic, another undid my

shoe-strings and dragged at them, the third, leader and director of the savage assault, actually worried my leg with its serrated beak. So, thinking it no time for nonsense, I dragged off a leg of the table, and armed with this weapon started belabouring the warlike creature. Nor was I satisfied with trifling blows, but avenged my hurt by killing the bird outright:

Such were the birds Herculean art subdued,
And with loud tumults to the skies pursued;
And such the Harpies the winged brothers chased
From trembling Phineus' illusive feast.
The heavens were startled at their clamorous flight,
And backward seemed to roll in wild affright.

I left the creature sprawling, while its companions, after picking up the beans that were scattered all about the floor, and finding themselves I suppose bereft of their leader, retreated into the Temple again. Then, proud of my booty and the vengeance I had exacted, I tossed the dead bird behind the bed, and washed the trifling wound in my leg with vinegar. Presently, fearing a scolding, I determined to be off, and gathering my belongings together started to leave the cottage. I had not yet crossed the threshold however when I saw Œnothea coming along with an earthen pot full of fire. I drew back again therefore, and throwing aside my robe, as if I had been waiting for her return, took my stand at the entrance. She packed her fire on some reeds broken up small, and piling up the top with a number of logs, began to excuse her delay, saying her friend had refused to let her go till she had drained the three cups custom required. Then, "What have you been doing," she asked, "in my absence? and where are the beans?"

I really thought I had done something very praiseworthy, and described the whole battle to her in detail, finally, to end her melancholy, presenting her with the dead goose in compensation for her loss. Directly the old woman set eyes on the bird, she set up such a terrible outcry you might have thought the geese had invaded the place again. Confused at this and astounded at the strange nature of my offence, I repeatedly begged her to tell me why she was so angry, and why all her pity was for the goose and none at all for me.

But beating her palms together, "How dare you speak," she screamed, "abandoned wretch! You must know what an atrocity you have committed; you have killed the delight of Priapus, the goose that was the darling of all the matrons. You think it's a trifle you've done!—if the Magistrates get wind of it, you'll be crucified. You polluted my home with blood, that was never profaned before; anl put it in the power of any ill-wisher I may have to turn me out of my office."

Trembling she spoke, and raging with despair,
She wounds her cheek, and rends her silver hair.
In copious streams fast flows the briny shower,
As down the hills the rapid torrents pour,
When Auster with indulgent softness blows,
Dissolves the frost and melts the mountain snows;
Thus in a flood of tears her eyes were drowned,
And from her inmost breast deep sighs resound.

"Don't shout so, I beseech you," I interposed; "I tell you, I'll give you an ostrich for your goose." She was still sitting on the pallet and bewailing the goose's untimely death, with me standing in amazement, when Proselenos arrived with the materials for the sacrifice. Directly she saw the dead bird, she asked excitedly how the calamity had occurred, and she too began to weep violently, and make as much ado over me as if I had killed my own father instead of a public goose. Feeling utterly sick of the tiresome business, "Now tell me," I expostulated, "could not I purchase expiation for money, if it was you I had assaulted, even though I'd done murder. Look you, I offer two gold pieces, enough to buy both gods and geese with." As soon as Œnothea saw the coins, "Forgive me, young man," she exclaimed; " 'tis for your sake I am so anxious, and that shows affection surely, not malice. (And we'll take care that no one shall know anything about it.) Only do you pray to the gods to pardon the sacrilege you have done."

Whoe'er has magic gold, secure may sail
Where'er he please, he's lord of Fortune's gale;
May in a Danae's arms make soft abode,—
There's no Acrisius will dispute the God!
He may turn Poet, Orator, what not?
When he harangues, old Cato is forgot!
Or if the noisy bar delights him more,
Behold what mighty Labeo was before!
In short—when of the money you're possessed,
You need but wish,—you've Jove within your chest.

Meantime the priestess, bustling about, placed a bowl of wine under my hands, and making me spread out my fingers evenly, purified them with leeks and parsley. Then with a muttered charm she dipped filberts in the wine, and accordingly as they rose to the surface again, or sank, she drew her prognostications. But I did not fail to observe that the blind nuts, with nothing but air inside instead of kernels, naturally floated on the top, while the heavy ones, that were full and sound within, settled to the bottom. Next turning her attentions to the goose, she opened its breast and drew out a fine fat liver, and proceeded to predict my future prospects from the indications it afforded. Nay! that not a trace of my crime might be left, she broke up the whole bird, and sticking the pieces on spits, prepared a very appetizing dinner for me, whom she had so short a time before condemned to death with her own lips. Meantime bumpers of unmixed wine were circulating freely, and the old woman merrily gobbled up the goose they had been mourning over so sadly just before. When it was all gone, the Priestess, now half drunk, turned to me and said, "We must complete the mysteries, to recover you of your impotency," and pounded nettle seed, and then proceeded to insert little by little up my anus. Next the cruel old dame anoints my two thighs with the same concoction. Then miche, which she smeared with oil and ground pepper.

So saying, Œnothea brought out a leathern gode-mixing nasturtium juice with southern-wood, she bathes my genitals with the stuff, and grasping a bundle of stinging nettles, begins slowly and methodically to lash my belly with them all over below the navel. The nettles burn sharply, and I suddenly take to my heels, the old women after me in hot haste. Though disordered with wine and lust, they take the right road, and follow me up through several streets, screaming, "Stop, thief!" However, I escaped eventually, after making all my toes bleed in the course of my headlong gallop.

CHAPTER SEVENTEEN

As soon as ever I could get home, I went to bed, utterly worn out with fatigue; but I was unable to sleep a wink. My various disasters kept on running through my head, and quite convinced I was the most unfortunate wretch alive, I ejaculated, "Fortune has ever been my bitterest foe; it only needed Love's torments as well to make me utterly miserable. Doomed wretch! Fortune and Love now join their forces to conspire my ruin. Cruel Cupid has never spared me; whether lover or loved, I am perpetually on the rack! There is Chrysis now! she loves me madly and never ceases to tease me. Chrysis who looked down on me, when she was acting as her mistress' go-between, and scorned me as a slave, because I wore slave's clothes, she, I say, that same Chrysis who once loathed my humble condition, is now bent on following it up even at the risk of life itself. She swore she would never leave me alone, that time she declared the vehemence of her passion for me.

"But Circe has my whole heart; all other women I despise. Indeed who so fair as she? What was Ariadne's beauty, or Leda's, compared to hers? What had Helen of Troy, or Venus herself, to boast against her? If Paris, umpire of the rival goddesses, had seen her at the trial with her dancing eyes, he would have given up all to her, Helen and the goddesses three! Could I but kiss that mouth, could I press that divine, that heavenly bosom, maybe my powers of body would return, and those parts of me revive that now lie torpid and, I verily believe, bewitched. No insults exhaust my patience. I have been thrashed,—'tis nothing; I have been kicked out,—'tis a merry jest; if only I may be restored to favour."

These and the like thoughts of lovely Circe's charms so roused my fancy that I disordered my bed with the repeated efforts of a sort of imaginary voluptuousness. But all my struggles remained unavailing. At last continual disappointment wore my patience out, and I cursed the evil enchantment that oppressed me. Presently however, recovering my self-control, and drawing what consolation I might from remembering how many heroes of antiquity had been persecuted by the anger of the gods, I broke out into these lines:

"Not I alone have Heaven's just anger felt,
The gods with others have severely dealt;
By Juno's rage the heavens Alcides bore,
And lost fair Hylas on the Pontic shore.
Laomedon did Jove's resentment feel,
And Telepus bled by the fatal steel.
Fate's sure decrees no mortal power can shun,
Nor can the swiftest from Heaven's vengeance run."

Tortured by these anxieties, I tossed about wakefully the whole night long. At peep of day Giton, informed of the fact of my having slept at home, entered my room, and after chiding me severely for my licentious way of life, told me the whole household were complaining bitterly of my goings on, how I paid scarcely any attention to business, and was like a ruin myself over the fatal intrigue I was now engaged in. I gathered from all this he was well posted in my affairs, and guessed some one had been to the house to inquire for me. I asked my companion if anyone had been in quest of me.

"No one to-day," Giton replied; "but yesterday there was a woman, stylishly dressed enough, came in, and after a long talk with me and boring me to death with her forced conversation, ended by saying you deserved the gallows and would surely get a slave's scourging, if the individual you had wronged persisted in his complaint." This news tormented me extremely, and I laughed out in fresh recrimination against Fortune. My invective was still in full swing when Chrysis came in, and throwing her arms wildly round my neck, exclaimed, "I have you in my arms, my heart's desire! My love, my joy! Never, never will you end this fire of mine, but by quenching it in my blood."

I was not a little disconcerted by this amorous display on her part, and resorted to a string of flattering speeches to get rid of her, fearing the madwoman's cries might reach Eumolpus's ears, who in the arrogance of success had now adopted the domineering ways of a real master. So I used every means to calm her excitement,—feigning love, whispering soft nothings; in a word, so cleverly did I play the fond adorer she thought me genuinely smitten with her charms. I explained what peril we should both be in, if she were caught with me in my bed-room, Eumolpus being only too ready to punish the smallest indiscretion. Hearing this, she left me hurriedly, all the more so as she saw Giton coming back, who had quitted the room shortly before she joined me.

Hardly was she gone before one of the newly engaged servants rushed in to tell me the master was excessively angry at my two days' neglect of my duties. The best thing I could do, he said, was to get some plausible excuse ready; for it was hardly possible his angry passions could subside without somebody getting a thrashing.

Giton seeing me so vexed and disheartened, did not say one word to me about the woman; he merely spoke of Eumolpus, recommending me to treat the matter jocularly with him, rather than look gloomy about it. I was glad enough to take his advice, and approached the old man with so gay an air that, instead of showing severity, he received me banteringly, rallying me about my success in love and complimenting me on my grace and elegance, which made me such a favourite with all the ladies. "It is no news to me," he went on, "that a most beautiful woman is dying of love for you; now this may very likely be useful to us on occasion, Encolpius. Well then! play the fond lover, you; I will keep up the same role I have been acting all along."

He was still speaking when a matron entered, a lady of the highest distinction, Philomela by name, who in earlier days had won many a fat legacy by the charms

of her youth; but who being old now and past her
prime, used to put her son and daughter in the way of
childless old men, and so continued to extend her old
trade by the efforts of these successors. Well! this
woman came to Eumolpus and proceeded to commend
her children to his judicious guardianship, and confide
herself and her hopes to his kindly good nature, asseverating he was the only man in all the world to train
young people by the daily inculcation of healthy precepts; in fine, that she was leaving her children under
Eumolpus's roof, that they might hear his words of
wisdom, the only heritage worth having that could be
bestowed on youth. And she was as good as her word;
for leaving behind her a very attractive looking girl
along with her brother, a stripling, in the old man's
chamber, she left the house under pretext of visiting
the Temple to say her prayers.

Eumolpus, who was so careful a soul he was ready
to take even me at my age for a minion, was not long
in inviting the girl to sacrifice to the rearward Venus.
But then he had informed everybody he was gouty and
crippled in the loins, and if he failed to keep up the
pretence, he ran considerable risk of spoiling the whole
play. So, to maintain the imposture intact, he begged
the girl to take a seat on that kindly good nature her
mother had appealed to, ordering Corax at the same
time to slip under the bed he lay on himself, and rest-
ing his hands on the floor, to hoist him up and down
with his back. The servant obeyed, and gently seconded the child's artful movements with a corre-
spondingly, rhythmical sea-saw. Then when the crisis

was coming, Eumolpus shouted out loud and clear to Corax to work faster. Thus the old fellow, suspended between his servant and his mistress, enjoyed himself as if in a swing. This exercise he repeated more than once, to the accompaniment of peals of laughter, in which he joined himself. Nor was I idle; but fearing my hand might get out of practice from disuse, I assailed the brother, where he stood admiring his sister's gymnastics through the key-hole, to see if he were amenable to outrage. Like a well trained lad, he made no bones about accepting my caresses; but once more, alas! I found the god unpropitious to my efforts.

However I was not so much cast down by failure this time as I had been on previous occasions; for very soon afterwards my vigour came back to me, and suddenly feeling myself in better condition, I exclaimed, "The great gods of higher heaven it is have made me a man again! Mercury, who conveys and re-conveys the souls of men, has of his loving-kindness given me back what an unfriendly hand had docked me of, to show you I am really more graciously endowed than ever was Protesilaus or any of the mighty men of yore." So saying, I lifted my tunic, and offered Eumolpus a view of all my glories. For an instant he stood panic-stricken; then, to make assurance doubly sure, he put out both hands and felt the good gift the gods had given me.

This great boon restoring our cheerfulness, we made merry over Philomela's artfulness and her children's proficiency, little likely to profit them much with us however; for it was solely and entirely in hopes of a legacy she had abandoned the boy and girl to our tender mercies. So reflecting on this sordid fashion of getting round childless old men, I was led on to think of the present state of our own fortunes, and took occasion to warn Eumolpus that this game of biting might easily end in biters being bit.

"Our every act," I added, "should be governed by caution. Socrates, wisest of mankind as both men and gods allow, was wont to boast he had never so much as glanced into a tavern, nor trusted his eyes to look at any crowded and disorderly assemblage. Nothing in the world is more advisable than always to speak within the bounds of prudence.

"All this is true," I insisted, "and no class of men is more liable to come to mischance than those who covet other folks' goods. How should mountebanks, and swindlers, live, unless they were now and again to toss a little purse or a jingling bag of money as baits to the crowd? Just as dumb beasts are enticed by food, so men are to be caught only with something solid in the way of expectations to bite at. The ship from Africa with your money and your slaves has not arrived, as you promised. Our fortune-hunters are tired out, and already stint their generosity. Either I am much mistaken, or the jade Fortune has begun to repent of her favours to you."

"I have thought out a scheme," Eumolpus replied, "that will mightily embarrass our fortune-hunting friends," and drawing his tablets from his wallet, he read out his last wishes as follows:

"All who shall receive legacies under my will, my

own freedom excepted, will inherit the said bequests subject to this condition, to wit, that they do cut up my body into pieces and eat the same before the eyes of the public there present.

"They need not be over and above shocked, I tell them; for we know that to this day some nations observe the custom by which the dead are eaten by their relatives—so much so indeed that sick folk amongst them are often reproached for spoiling their flesh by being so long ill. I remind my friends of these facts, that they may not refuse to follow my directions, but rather consume my dead body with the same heartiness with which they prayed the living breath might leave it."

Just as he was reading the initial clauses, several of Eumolpus's most intimate friends came into his room, and seeing the document in his hand, begged him eagerly to let them hear its contents. He consented instantly, and read it out from beginning to end. On hearing the extraordinary stipulation about being obliged to eat his corpse, they were very much cast down. But the glamour of his wealth so dazzled the wretched creatures and stifled their consciences, making mere cringing cowards of them in his presence that they durst enter no protest against the enormity. One of them, however, Gorgias, was ready to comply, provided he had not too long to wait.

At this Eumolpus continued, turning to Gorgias, "I have no apprehensions of your stomach's turning rebellious; it will obey orders, once you promise it, in return for one hour's nausea, a plethora of good things. Just shut your eyes, and pretend it's not human flesh you've bolted, but a cool ten million. Besides, we'll find some condiments, never fear, to disguise the flavour. Indeed no meat really tastes good by itself, but is always masked in some artful way, and the recalcitrant stomach reconciled to it. Why! if you want examples to fortify your resolutions—the Saguntines, when hard pressed by Hannibal, ate human flesh; and they had no legacy to expect. The men of Perusia did the same thing in the extremity of famine, looking for no other benefit from the horrid diet but just to escape starvation. When Numantia was taken by Scipio, mothers were found grasping their children's half-eaten bodies to their bosoms. In fine, seeing it is merely the idea of cannibalism that can cause disgust, you must fight with all your heart to banish this repugnance from your minds, to the end you may receive the enormous legacies I put you down for."

These insolent extravagances Eumolpus reeled off with such reckless inconsequence as made the fortune hunters begin to distrust his promises. Instantly they began to scrutinize more closely our words and actions, and everything they saw only increasing their suspicions, they soon set us down for a gang of common cheats and swindlers. Hereupon such as had gone to more than ordinary expense for our entertainment, resolved to have at us and take their just revenge.

But now Chrysis, who was in all their secrets, warned me of what the Crotonians' intentions toward us were. This news scared me so terribly I fled instantly with Giton, leaving Eumolpus to his fate; and a few days later I learned that the Crotonians, furious at the old fox having lived sumptuously at their expense for so long, had massacred him in the Massilian fashion. To show you what this means, I must tell you that whenever the Massilians were visited by the Plague, one of the poorer inhabitants would volunteer himself as an expiatory victim, on condition of being maintained a full year at the public cost and fed on choice food. Later on, the unhappy man, bedecked with festal wreaths and sacred robes, was carried in procession through the whole city, and made the butt of general execration, to the end that all the calamities of all the State might be concentrated on his devoted head. This done, he was hurled headlong from a rock.

THE END